Hope C

Christmas magic on the children's ward!

It's a time of miracles and magic—and as
Hope Children's Hospital prepares to celebrate its first
Christmas in the historic city of Cambridge, England,
the staff will do everything they can to make their
little patients' wishes come true.

Billionaire CEO Theo Hawkwood leads a
world-renowned handpicked medical team who strive
to give the best treatment to their precious charges,
and hope to all who come through the doors.
This Christmas, they'll discover that miracles can
be found in the most unexpected of places—and love
will prove the greatest gift of all!

Their Newborn Baby Gift by Alison Roberts
One Night, One Unexpected Miracle by Caroline Anderson

Available now!

The Army Doc's Christmas Angel by Annie O'Neil
The Billionaire's Christmas Wish by Tina Beckett

Coming December 2018!

Dear Reader,

When my editor asked me to write this book as part of a miniseries, I hesitated briefly, because it's been a long time since I wrote a book in conjunction with other authors and I wasn't sure who I'd be working with. I needn't have worried! I ended up with the wonderful Alison Roberts, Annie O'Neil and Tina Beckett, and they were fabulous. It made such a change, because writing is a very solitary occupation, and sharing parts of that process with fellow authors was a delight. Annie and I had great fun dreaming up Doodle, the therapy dog, and I got a sneak preview of Alison's and Annie's books to make sure I picked up all the threads and handed them on intact—hopefully without too many glaring errors!

And of course it wasn't all collaboration. I still had my own story to tell, the gradual unfolding of a love to last a lifetime. Marco and Alice gave me a few headaches on the way, but we got there in the end, and I left them both in a much happier place. Say hi to them for me, and give Doodle and Wuzzle a cuddle on the way past, please. I'm missing them already!

Caroline x

ONE NIGHT, ONE UNEXPECTED MIRACLE

———

CAROLINE ANDERSON

HARLEQUIN® MEDICAL ROMANCE™

Special thanks and acknowledgment are given
to Caroline Anderson for her contribution to the
Hope Children's Hospital series.

Recycling programs
for this product may
not exist in your area.

ISBN-13: 978-1-335-66383-2

One Night, One Unexpected Miracle

First North American Publication 2018

Copyright © 2018 by Harlequin Books S.A.

Printed in U.S.A.

Books by Caroline Anderson

Harlequin Medical Romance

Yoxburgh Park Hospital

From Christmas to Eternity
The Secret in His Heart
Risk of a Lifetime
Their Meant-to-Be Baby
The Midwife's Longed-For Baby
Bound by Their Babies
Their Own Little Miracle

Harlequin Romance

The Valtieri Baby
Snowed in with the Billionaire
Best Friend to Wife and Mother?

Visit the Author Profile page
at Harlequin.com for more titles.

For Alison Roberts, Annie O'Neil and
Tina Beckett, three fabulous ladies it was a
privilege to work with. Love you all xxx

PROLOGUE

HE COULDN'T TAKE his eyes off her.

He'd had to for a moment while he was tied up with Ryan Walker, the new neonatal cardiac surgeon who'd arrived in the UK just in time for the gala opening of Hope Children's Hospital. Theo Hawkwood, the CEO, had asked him to introduce Ryan to people at the party, but he'd skilfully palmed him off on the head of ICU so now he was free to indulge himself again and, man, was it worth it.

She looked stunning.

What a contrast from her usual scrubs, which hung on her petite body and did a great job of hiding what he now realised was an amazing figure.

From all the time she spent in the gym when she was off duty? It wasn't his thing, he liked the great outdoors, but he'd heard she was constantly either in the gym or in the pool, swimming for an hour at a time, and occasionally when he'd been out running in the early morning he'd seen her leave her house in tracksuit and trainers. Going to the gym, probably, and whatever she did there obviously worked.

Not for him. He hated being trapped in a room filled with pumping music and sweaty bodies. He'd grown up amongst the slopes of the family vineyards in Tuscany, and although the city of Cambridge was set in a flat landscape with barely a wrinkle, it made for good running, so he ran every morning, rain or shine, pushing himself to the limit, and sometimes his route took him past her house as he pounded the footpaths by the river and the bridleways out into the countryside.

Now, though, the only thing pounding was his heart, the heavy thud as he studied her beating in his ears. Her dress was blue, the same astonishingly brilliant blue as her eyes, and it clung to her slender frame like a second skin. It shimmered in the lights, showing every curve and hollow, so that even though the neck was high and the sleeves elbow length—typical Alice, all demure and buttoned up like a Victorian schoolmarm—it left little to the imagination.

She glanced across at him, her eyes locking briefly with his through the crowd, and he lifted his glass to her, feeling the tension that was always between them tighten like an invisible thread that ran across the room and connected them together.

It had been like that since the first day, this *thing* that hovered in the background so that even if he couldn't see her, he knew when she was near him. Was it the same for her? He thought so. He'd caught the odd glimpse, a little flash of something quickly hidden, an inner battle with herself which she always seemed to win.

Like now.

She'd held his eyes for a fraction, then coolly turned away, winning the battle of wills with herself again, but the tension stayed with him like a knot in his chest.

Was she still angry with him? Maybe. She had reason to be, because he'd really pushed it this morning and the tension was tighter now than ever, the verbal sparring that had been business as usual for them since day one for some reason escalating today without warning.

They'd taken it to a whole new level, and he didn't really understand why. When they were operating, they moved like clockwork, reading each other's minds, two halves of a whole, and neither of them ever criticised the other's clinical ability or judgement. But Alice Baxter was his boss, and outside the operating theatre she did things a certain way and expected him to do the same.

Which he didn't. Not always, at least, and sometimes he deliberately didn't just to get a rise out of her. Like today. And he teased her and flirted with her for the same reason. Was that why she'd lost it with him? That he'd gone too far just to ramp up the tension and push her to the limit?

He'd been going to apologise, but then she'd been so cutting, so short with him that he'd gone all macho Italian male on her and then stalked off because it was either that or kiss her, which was so massively unprofessional and out of line that even he, with his cheerful disregard for convention, had backed away.

Yes, he really needed to apologise.

Then someone in the crowd moved, giving him a perfect view of her, and he nearly choked on his prosecco.

The dress was backless.

Well, not entirely, of course, but backless enough to take his breath away and send his heart into overdrive. A fine strand of fabric was held together by a sparkling clasp at the nape of her slender neck, and below it the pale, smooth skin of her back was bracketed by shimmering blue, plunging all the way down to her hips, reuniting to caress the subtle curve of her bottom.

He swallowed. His hands ached to cup that sweet curve, to pull her up against his body, to feel those surprisingly generous breasts against his chest…

Time to put things back on an even keel. He'd flirted outrageously with her this morning, but he didn't want to flirt with her now. Not any more. He wanted more than that, something else entirely, something much, much more serious.

A relationship?

Never going to happen. She was his boss, and his feelings were totally inappropriate.

But not unreciprocated, unless he'd read her wrong? Yes, they wrangled constantly, but under it all was this quiet simmer of emotion, attraction, sensuality—call it what you will, it was there in every moment of every day, unless they were operating. Well, they weren't operating now, and maybe it was time to confront this, to apologise and get things back to normal.

He put his empty glass down on a passing tray and headed across the room.

He was watching her. She could feel it, feel the stroke of his eyes over the bare skin of her back like a caress, and the conversation around her was dead to her ears. All she could think about, all she could feel, was Marco watching her across the room.

She always knew when he was there, could always feel his presence, knew he was coming even before she heard his voice. It was like some sort of sixth sense—a sense she could gladly have done without because it was playing hell with her work life and even creeping into her dreams.

And last night the dreams had been definitely X-rated…

She laughed when the others did, took another gulp of prosecco and nearly choked on the bubbles. What was *wrong* with her tonight? It was all just because of that stupid dream, and she could still feel the touch of his hands on her body—

Ridiculous. Sheer fantasy. There was no way anything was going to happen between them, even if he did flirt constantly with her.

That was just Marco, and it didn't mean anything. He flirted with every female with a pulse, from the babies up to the great-grandmothers visiting their tiny relatives, and he had them all eating out of the palm of his hand.

He probably didn't even realise he was doing it, it was as natural as breathing—and to be fair it wasn't so much flirting as just breaking the ice and gentle teasing. Unless it was her.

Then there was an undercurrent of sensuality that, try as she might, she couldn't ignore.

Because she didn't *want* to ignore it? Wanted to call him out on it, see if he really meant what he said? But she wouldn't, of course, for all sorts of reasons, not least cowardice. What if she was reading much more into it than was actually there? Although it had certainly been there in her dream.

She sighed crossly, stopped pretending to listen to the conversation she should have been part of and excused herself.

She needed some air. Preferably cold and bracing and strong enough to blow some common sense into her before she did something stupid.

She was his *boss*, for goodness' sake! She couldn't let herself give in to it—which was why she'd ripped his head off earlier when he'd been pushing her buttons, and he'd drawn himself up and gone all Italian male on her and made it even worse, but it had been her fault. She'd started it by overreacting and she ought to apologise—

'Alice.'

Even her name was a caress on his lips. She closed her eyes briefly, annoyed that her radar had failed to warn her that he was coming. Marco Ricci, her unbelievably sexy, unbelievably annoying and insubordinate subordinate. Except that had sexual connotations, and there was no room for any of that in their relationship and she was keeping it that way if it killed her.

Which it might.

She sucked in a breath, plastered a noncommittal smile on her lips and turned to face him.

'Marco. Did you want me?'

Stupid! Stupid, stupid, stupid!

Something flitted through his eyes and was gone, but his lips had twitched and she braced herself for the smart retort.

'Nothing that won't keep. You look beautiful tonight, Alice,' he murmured, his voice like rough silk teasing her nerve endings.

She felt a wash of colour sweep up her throat and she looked away, shocked by the hitch in her heart rate and her body's reaction to that deep, rich, slightly accented voice and the slow caress of his eyes that had left fire in its wake.

She was used to him flirting with her, but he wasn't flirting now. The look in his eyes and the tone of his voice went far beyond that and called to something deep inside her, long repressed, cold and lonely and desperate for attention.

'Thank you,' she muttered, and swallowed hard. 'You don't look so bad yourself.'

Understatement of the century. He was sexy enough in scrubs. In a beautifully cut tux that showed off broad, solid shoulders to perfection, with the sharp contrast of the blinding white dress shirt against olive skin darkened by the shadow of stubble, those dark-lashed eyes simmering with latent heat, he was jaw-droppingly, unsettlingly gorgeous and she felt the impact of it in every yearning cell of her body.

'So—Evie's done a brilliant job organising this,' she added hurriedly, hauling her eyes off him and groping for something uncontroversial. 'I wouldn't have believed the conference hall could be turned into such an amazing ballroom.'

'No,' he said, not taking his eyes from her face. Not that she was looking at him, but she could still feel the steady, searching gaze of those magnetic eyes and her pulse was rocketing.

She was trying to find something to say to fill the yawning void when the music started, and to her surprise he held out his hand to her.

'Come. Dance with me. We've been fighting all day about nothing and it's time to stop.'

'Is that an apology?'

She made herself meet his eyes again, and for a fleeting instant she thought she saw regret. No. Marco never regretted anything, he wasn't made like that. She'd imagined it. Of course it wasn't an apology.

'Yes, it's an apology,' he said softly, his Italian accent suddenly stronger. 'Dance with me,

Alice. Life's serious enough. It's time to have some fun.'

Fun? She hadn't let herself have *fun* in years. At least, not the sort of fun she thought he was talking about.

Eyes steady, he took the glass out of her hand, handed it to one of the circulating bar staff and led her to the dance floor, turning her into his arms. She felt the heat of his hand on her bare back, the other still holding hers, curled loosely between them by her shoulder. Normally her head was level with his chest, but she was wearing heels tonight and her eyes were right by his immaculately knotted bow tie. Above it she could see the throb of a pulse beating in his throat, and he tilted his head so his cheek was against her forehead as he drew her closer.

She could smell cologne, just a faint touch of something exotic, something dangerously enticing that seemed to enter her bloodstream and invade every part of her as she swayed to the music. The hand on her back slid down, down to the base of her spine, his fingers splayed against her skin as he eased her closer still.

Too close for her sanity. Close enough to bring back the dream—

She took a step back out of his arms.

'I need some air,' she said breathlessly, and, turning, she made her way quickly off the crowded dance floor and out of the conference hall, her body on fire with a need she'd never felt before, hadn't even known existed.

The lift? She couldn't run downstairs in her heels, so there was no choice, and the lift was standing there waiting…

He watched her retreat for a nanosecond, then followed her, carving his way through the crowd, the white-blonde of her hair easy to pick out when he could find it, but even in those heels she wasn't tall and the room was full and he kept losing her.

The doors. She was heading for the doors, and then the lift. He cut off the corner, went through another set of doors and reached the hallway just as the lift doors started to close.

Good job he was fit. He sprinted across the landing from a standing start, slammed his hand into the gap and pushed the doors open again.

She turned and met his eyes furiously—or desperately?

'What are you doing?' she demanded, but her voice sounded odd, a little frantic.

He hit the button to close the doors. 'What does it look like? I'm following you.'

'Why?'

Her voice was breathless, a slight catch in it, and he smiled a little grimly. 'Because I need to apologise properly. Not just about the fighting, but about this, too.'

He stabbed the button for the ground floor and folded his arms just to stop himself reaching out to her.

'What *this*? I don't understand.'

He sighed again. 'Yes, you do, Alice, because it's just here, between us, all the time,' he told her, waving his hand back and forth between them, 'and it's getting in the way of our work. We need to talk about it.'

'You're imagining it,' she said, but she couldn't hold his eyes, and he unfolded his arms and reached out and turned her head gently to face him.

'Am I?' he murmured. 'Am I really? I don't think so, Alice. I think you want me as much as I want you, and what we have to do is work out how we're going to deal with it, because we have to, one way or the other, because it's getting in the way all the time and it can't go on like this.'

It was there again in his eyes, that flash of something she'd seen just before he'd asked her to dance, briefly pushed aside by regret but back again now, with bells on.

Heat. Smouldering heat in the black depths of his eyes, his pupils flared, his chest rising and falling as he studied her silently, those eyes reeling her in.

'Why would you want me?' she asked, her voice annoyingly breathless again. 'Of all the women in this hospital, why me, Marco?'

His eyebrows shot up. '*Why?* Because you're beautiful and sexy and funny and sharp and clever and—because you keep your distance, button yourself up, bottle up everything that I can see raging inside you, and all I can think about is unbuttoning all those tiny little buttons holding you together and seeing what would happen if I set those feelings free.'

Set them free? The thought terrified her, because he was right, they *were* there, raging inside her, and every day, every minute, every time she saw him, this beautiful, magnificent, tempestuous, arrogant man, she wanted him.

And it was *never* going to happen—

'You're wrong. You don't really want me,' she whispered, but he just laughed and took her hand and pressed it firmly against his chest so she could feel the pounding of his heart.

'Can you feel that, *cara*? Can you feel how I want you? Always,' he murmured, his eyes softening, 'every minute of every day,' and then he lowered his head, his hands cradling her face, just as the lift pinged a warning.

He wrenched his head up and moved away,

slid his hand down her arm and threaded his fingers through hers, nodded to the people waiting to go up and walked with her briskly out of the lift, across the central foyer and into the consulting room area.

He pulled his lanyard out of his pocket, swiped the security lock with the magnetic card and opened the doors, then pushed the nearest consulting room door open and ushered her through it.

She heard it click shut, then nothing, just the suspense that swirled around them in the air and robbed her brain of oxygen.

What did he want from her?

A deep, slow sigh cut through the silence and she heard the examination couch creak behind her as he sat on it.

'What do we do, Alice?' he asked, his voice low and, oh, so sexy, unravelling her rigid self-control and leaving her open and vulnerable.

'I don't know. What do you want from me, Marco?'

He laughed softly, and the sound teased her nerve endings and sent shivers of need through her body. 'I have no idea. Well, I have, but that's not going to happen, we both know that.'

Was that regret in his voice? She couldn't tell without looking into his eyes, so she turned and searched them, and then wished she hadn't because the humour, the teasing that seemed to dance almost permanently in them was gone, leaving something far more dangerous to her self-control and peace of mind.

Desire, white-hot and irresistible. She swallowed and took a step back, bumping into the desk and sitting down abruptly on the edge of it before her legs gave out.

'So what do we do?'

He laughed again, a wry huff of sound that unravelled her a little further, then met her eyes again.

'I don't know, but I know we can't go on like this, fighting all the time about nothing and dancing round the elephant in the room. I want you, Alice, and I don't seem to be able to put that on one side, and I don't think you can, either.'

His eyes held her, the need in them so openly expressed she was in no doubt about it. He wasn't toying with her. He really meant it, and his words had so accurately expressed her own feelings that she felt as if he could see into her soul.

He was right. She couldn't put it on one side, couldn't ignore it any longer. Didn't *want* to ignore it any longer.

As if he saw the moment she crumbled, he held out his hand silently, and she stood up, her legs shaking, and walked over to him, taking his hand and letting him draw her up against him, standing between his legs as he was propped on the edge of the couch, his warmth enclosing her.

He raised a hand and traced the line of her jaw, lifting a stray lock of hair away and tucking it back behind her ear. The caress was so tender, so gentle that it made her want to cry. It had been so long since anyone had touched her like that, as if she was something precious and fragile. If ever…

She met his eyes again, and he stared into hers for an age, then drew her nearer, lowered his head and touched his lips to hers.

She moaned softly against his mouth, parting her lips to him, and she felt his hands cradle her cheeks as he deepened the kiss. She met him touch for touch, stroke for stroke, their tongues searching, duelling.

They always duelled, but not like this, not—

'Marco…'

'I want you, Alice,' he groaned softly. 'Tell me you want me, too.'

'No—yes— Marco, I—'

'Alice, you're killing me…'

He kissed her again, his lips coaxing, trailing fire down her throat, over her shoulders, in that delicate, sensitive place behind her ear. She arched her neck to give him better access, his name a sob in her throat. 'Marco…'

'Tell me, Alice,' he said, his voice low, scraping over her senses like gravel and bringing everything to life. 'Tell me you want me. Tell me you want this, too, before I go crazy—'

'Yes.'

'Yes, what?'

'Yes, I want you. *I want you…*'

He muttered something in Italian and his hands reached down, bunching up her dress as his mouth plundered hers and his body rocked against her, pressing her up against him. She could feel his hands on her skin, cradling her bottom, sliding up around her waist as he lifted her easily and turned, settling her on the edge of the examination couch where he had been.

Her legs wrapped around his waist, holding him tightly against her, the pressure building as her fingers found the ends of his bow tie and tugged it undone. She couldn't do the buttons, her fingers were shaking too much, and with a little scream of frustration she ripped his shirt open, her nails raking down his chest in the process.

'*Dio*, Alice—'

He buried his hands in her hair and rocked against her, his body tight against her most intimate places as his mouth took hers again, his tongue searching, delving, and she wanted him closer. Needed him closer. Needed him…

'I want you,' she said, her breath hissing out between her teeth. 'Marco, please, now. I want you—'

He swore softly and pulled away a fraction. 'Don't move.'

She dropped her head back and closed her eyes, the breath shuddering out of her body as he let her go and stepped away, and she clenched her legs together against the raging need and waited. She could hear him doing something, heard the snap of a wallet, the soft rasp of a zip, a slight rustle.

A condom. Of all the tragic ironies. She nearly laughed, only it wasn't funny. He didn't need it—except to protect her and himself from the other unintended consequences of random sex. Nothing else…

She opened her eyes and moaned again, her body throbbing with need as she reached for him, gripping the firm shaft of his erection and sliding her hand down it, unrolling the condom along its length. He swore softly in Italian and eased away the scrap of silk that passed for her underwear, his hips nudging her legs apart again as he slid his fingers deep inside her.

She gasped and tried to clench her legs together to quell the waves of sensation but there was no way because he was there, his body filling her at last, making her sob with need as he thrust into her, slowly at first and then faster, harder, again and again, his hands cradling her bottom and holding her tight against him, rocking as her control splintered into pieces and she convulsed around him.

He caught her cry in his mouth, his body tensing, shuddering with the force of his climax, and then as it passed he let out a long, fractured sigh, dropped his head against her shoulder and cradled her close, his mouth against her ear murmuring soft words she didn't understand.

She couldn't speak, couldn't think, couldn't move. Her body was a seething mass of sensation so intense that even now she could feel the shockwaves rippling through her, and as he finally eased away she couldn't look at him.

What had she done?

She'd *never* felt like that. Never responded like that, so wildly, so spontaneously, so freely it had felt like she was flying.

Not now, though. Not any more.

Now she'd come down to earth with a bump, crippled with self-consciousness, and she slid off the edge of the couch, rescued her underwear from the floor and pulled it on hastily. As she tugged her dress straight with shaking hands, she felt a nail catching on the delicate fabric.

'*Cara?*'

Gentle fingers caught her chin, lifting her face up so he could read her eyes, and he sighed and drew her back into his arms. 'You're buttoning up again,' he murmured, his voice heavy with regret, and she tried to push him away.

'I have to. I'm your *boss,* Marco! I can't just sleep with you—'

'Who said anything about sleeping? I think we were both wide awake just then. And don't even try and tell me you didn't enjoy it.'

She didn't. She wasn't a liar, and he'd only laugh at her anyway.

'It was a mistake,' she said, knowing instantly that he'd argue, but he didn't. Instead he bent his head and kissed her tenderly, nearly trashing her resolve.

'Yes. It was. You deserved better than a—' He broke off, and she could almost see him rearranging the words in his mouth. 'I should have taken you for dinner, taken you back to my house and made love to you slowly, for hours. Explored every part of you, kissed every inch of your skin, made you come for me again and again and again—'

'It would still have been a mistake,' she said, her insides weeping at the thought of him loving her so thoroughly, so tenderly, so meticulously. 'We can't do this, Marco. I agree we have to find a way to work together without fighting, but this isn't it. This isn't the way. We can't do it again.'

She stood motionless, and after a second or two his arms dropped and he stepped back, glanced down at his ripped shirt with a rueful smile, shrugged and opened the door.

'I'm sorry. Not for doing it. I can't regret that. But if that's what you want it won't happen again, I promise you. Goodnight, Alice.'

And with that he walked out, headed through the door at the end and left her standing there wondering what on earth she'd done, and why it suddenly felt as if, by letting him go, she'd thrown away a chance at happiness that she hadn't even known was there…

CHAPTER ONE

Five weeks later...

'Do you want me to close?'

'What, because you imagine you can do it better than me?'

His eyes crinkled above his mask. 'Because I *know* I can do it better than you,' he said, and she could hear the smile in his voice. It was odd, but since that night five weeks ago their sparring had changed to a mutual and much more gentle teasing, almost as if they'd called a truce and were carefully tiptoeing around each other's feelings. Even his flirting had toned down, which was a shame. She almost missed it, but she knew why he'd done it. It was too dangerous now, after what had happened. It would be fanning the flames of a fire that had to be allowed to die. A fire that hadn't, sadly, burned itself out.

'You're so arrogant,' she said mildly, stepping

away and stripping off her gloves. She tried so hard not to smile, but he just chuckled as if he could see it and held out his hand to the scrub nurse.

'Three-oh Prolene, please,' he said, and the nurse placed the suture in his hand and he dropped his eyes and began meticulously drawing the wound edges together, layer by layer.

He was right, he was better than her at suturing, but only by a hair and she had a feeling it was a simple matter of Italian pride that prevented him from failing. And not to be better than her would be failure in his eyes.

She dragged her gaze away. She couldn't watch him, couldn't watch those sensitive, intelligent hands delicately repairing the boy's abdomen. So skilful. So focused. Just as they'd been on her body—

'I'll go and talk to his parents.'

'OK. Just don't take all the credit.'

'Only where it's due.'

She turned away, stripped off her mask and hat and gown and went to change. She would talk to Amil's parents, tell them how it had gone, and then she had things to do, a patient to see, letters to write to parents, some results to review. She couldn't just stand around looking at him simply because he was poetry in motion. Too dangerous. She was trying to keep her distance, and watching him wouldn't help that at all.

And besides, there was something else she had to do. Something pressing. Something she'd never thought she'd need to do, and couldn't quite believe. Couldn't *dare* to believe.

She had to do a pregnancy test, because this morning she'd made herself a coffee and she'd been unable to drink it. She'd sipped it, but it had sat in her stomach like a rock and she'd had to rinse her mouth to get rid of the taste.

Maybe she'd just had too much coffee over the years and her body had started to rebel? But she was hungry, too, and although she was used to that, almost welcomed it because it was a good sign in her case, today she felt a little light-headed and woozy. And her periods, never as regular as clockwork, were an unreliable sign, but even so it had been a while.

So while he was working miracles on the child's skin, she spoke to the boy's parents, went to her locker, got out the test kit she'd bought on the way to work and went to the ladies' loo.

It wouldn't be positive. It couldn't be. Her body didn't do ovulation—couldn't do it, because her ovaries were stupid.

PREGNANT

She stared at the wand for a good five minutes before she moved, her mind in freefall.

She was pregnant with Marco's baby.

How? It *couldn't* have happened. There was no *way* she could have conceived, and besides, he'd used a condom! But one of her nails had snagged her dress as she'd tugged it straight afterwards. Just a tiny jagged edge where she must have caught it on something. When she'd shredded his shirt and raked her nails across that strong, solid expanse of chest? Could that have been enough? And when she'd reached down and touched him right after that, helped him put the condom on, had her nail torn it maybe?

It seemed so unlikely—but what other explanation was there?

None. And, however it had happened, however unbelievable it was, it was definitely Marco's baby, so she'd have to tell him, but how?

She closed her eyes, squeezing them hard against the well of mixed emotions, and pressed her hand over her mouth. How would he react? Would he be angry? She hoped not. Delighted? Unlikely. And then a chilling thought crossed her mind. Would he want her to keep it, or—?

No. She'd seen him with children. There was no way he'd want that. He was an Italian, and children were at the front and centre of their world. They were for her, too, which was why she'd chosen paediatrics, because it was the closest she'd thought she'd ever come to having children.

Until now. And now, totally unexpectedly, right out of the blue, she was having a baby. The thing she'd dreamed of and longed for and tried to put out of her mind ever since she'd been told it might never happen for her *was* happening, but she daren't invest too much of herself in it because she knew there was a distinct possibility it might all go wrong, because it would be considered a high-risk pregnancy.

Pregnancy. A word she'd never thought she'd use in association with herself, certainly not now in her late thirties, and as she sifted through the blizzard of emotions whirling through her, she didn't know how she felt about it.

Thrilled? Shocked? Or just plain terrified?

All of them. And add sick to that.

'How's Amil?'

'Fine. He's in Recovery, looking good. They're moving him to PICU shortly and the anaesthetist is going to keep his pain relief topped up with the epidural so he should feel much better soon. I spoke to the parents again, filled them in a bit more.' He cocked his head on one side. 'How about you? Get your admin done?'

Admin? She hadn't even been in her office. 'Some of it,' she said—which, if you counted finding out if you'd need maternity leave as 'admin', wasn't a lie. 'We need to talk.'

'About a patient? I've got time now.'

'No. Not about a patient. About—us.'

His right eyebrow climbed into his hair. *'Us?'*

She held his eyes silently and with a huge effort, and he shrugged.

'Sure. How about this evening over dinner? I know a nice little Italian restaurant. They do great pasta.'

Pasta. Hunger and nausea warred, and hunger won. 'That sounds good. What time? Do we need to book?'

'No. Seven?'

She nodded. 'I'll meet you there.'

'No. I'll pick you up.'

'You don't know where I live.'

'Yes, I do. I run past your house some mornings, and I've seen you coming out in your gym kit on your way to the hospital.'

He ran past her house? Why had she never seen him? Or had she, maybe, once or twice, and not realised who he was? There were plenty of runners in the morning. She often saw them. He must be one of them.

'So—shall I come for you at ten to seven?

The restaurant's not far from you, it'll only take a few minutes to get there on foot.'

'Ten to seven is fine. Now I need to go and make some calls and write a couple of letters. I'll see you later.'

He didn't see much of her for the rest of the day, which was just as well because he didn't know what to think and she'd only distract him. She always distracted him, unless he was operating. Then he was focused, but otherwise…

They should never have done what they did at the gala. Not that he regretted it, not a bit, and things between them had been easier since, in a way. She'd been less on his case about everything, but he wanted more than they'd had that night, much more, and he knew she didn't. She'd made that perfectly clear, and he had to respect that, but the memories were playing hell with his sleep and he kept imagining her with him, sharing his bed, sharing his house—sharing his life? Never going to happen, he'd told himself, and now this.

This wanting to talk to him about 'us'. What 'us'? Was there going to be an 'us'?

It drove him crazy for the rest of the day, so it was a good job he was busy checking on his post-op patients, ending with Amil Khan in PICU, and he spent a long time talking to the boy's parents about his condition going forward. One of Theo Hawkwood's pro bono cases, the boy had Crohn's disease, and so far he hadn't been in remission. Maybe they could turn it round for him at last, and this op to remove a section of badly damaged bowel had at least given him a chance of recovery. And he hadn't needed a stoma, so he wouldn't need a bag, which was good news.

It was after six before he left them, and he ran home, showered rapidly and got to her house a minute late. She opened her door and for once didn't comment on his timekeeping. And she looked—nervous? Why? If she was going to suggest they had an affair, he was more than willing. And they were working better together, so it wasn't that…

'Ready?'

She nodded, and he stepped back and held open the little gate at the end of her path, then fell into step beside her as they walked into the centre and turned down a narrow, cobbled street, and as they walked he told her a little about the restaurant.

'This place is a gem. I found it when I first moved here seventeen years ago, and it's still run by the same family, but the son's taken over and he's every bit as good as his father. I eat here often because the food's healthy and it's delicious and it reminds me of home.'

'I'm surprised we didn't have to book if it's that good.'

'They were expecting me tonight anyway. Here we are.'

He opened the door and held it for her, and as she walked in she hesitated and he nearly bumped into her.

'Are you OK?'

She nodded, her pale hair bobbing brightly in the atmospheric lighting. 'Yes, I'm fine.'

No, she wasn't, but he couldn't work out why and then he didn't have time because the old man was walking towards him with a beaming smile, addressing him by name as he always did, showing them to their table, taking her coat, telling them about the specials.

'Alice?'

'I just want something simple,' she said quickly. 'Something fairly plain and light.'

'My son cooks a wonderful fish linguine,' Renzo said. 'That's light and delicate with a touch of fresh chilli.'

'Just a touch?'

'I can ask him to put less.'

She nodded. 'Thank you. And could I have some iced water, please?'

'I'll have the same. It's a great dish. And a glass of house white, Renzo. *Grazie mille.*'

He watched Renzo walk away, then propped his elbows on the table and searched her eyes, his patience finally at an end. 'So—this "us" you wanted to talk about…'

She wasn't sure she did. Not now, not here where he had friends. And she wasn't sure the restaurant was a great idea for another reason, either. One she hadn't even thought of, stupidly.

'Alice?'

She'd looked down, knotting her hands on the edge of the table, unsure how she felt, but now she made herself look up and meet his searching brown eyes. 'It's about what—happened.'

'The gala.'

She nodded and swallowed. 'I—um—it seems it's had…'

'Had…?'

She dropped her eyes again, unable to hold that searching gaze while she groped for the word. 'Consequences,' she said at last, and held her breath.

He said nothing. Not for at least thirty seconds, maybe even a minute. Then he reached out slowly, tipped up her face with gentle fingers and gave her a slightly bemused smile.

'You're pregnant?' he mouthed.

She nodded. 'Yes. Apparently I am.'

He leant forward, his voice low. 'But—how? I was careful.'

'I know. I'm not sure. I might have broken a nail when I—when I ripped your shirt. Maybe that…'

'Your nail? But…'

She could see him scrolling through what they'd done in those few frantic minutes, and saw the moment the light dawned.

He swore softly in Italian, then took her hands in his and held them firmly. 'I am so sorry. I never meant that to happen, but of course it changes everything.'

'Everything?'

'*Sì*. Because we're definitely an "us" now. I can't walk away from this.'

'But it may not even—'

They were interrupted by the arrival of the steaming, fragrant linguine. Renzo set a plate down in front of Alice, and as he turned away she felt her colour drain.

She pushed back her chair and stumbled to her feet. 'I'm sorry. I can't—I'm really sorry—'

Then she grabbed her bag and ran, not even waiting for her coat because if she didn't get out it was going to be hideously embarrassing.

She headed home, half running, half stumbling on the cobbles, and as she reached her house and let herself in, the nausea swamped her and she fled for the bathroom.

He knocked on the door, rang the bell, knocked again, and then finally he heard her coming down the stairs.

He'd known she was in because the lights were on upstairs and they hadn't been before, but when she opened the door she was as white as a sheet and trembling and he was racked with guilt.

'Alice,' he said softly, and stepped inside, closing the door behind him and putting the bag and her coat down on the floor to take her into his arms. 'I'm so sorry. If I'd known I would never have suggested going there. Come on, you need to sit down.'

'Did you bring my coat?'

'Yes. And I brought our food. Renzo put it in boxes for me.'

'I can't—'

'You can. You must. You need carbs, *cara*. Trust me, I grew up surrounded by pregnant women and I know what works.'

He left her on the sofa, arms wrapped round her slender frame and looking miserable and strangely afraid, and he headed down the hall towards what had to be the kitchen. He'd never seen her anything but confident, so why was she afraid? Afraid of what? Of him, his reaction? Of being pregnant? Of having a child? Maybe he'd misread it. Maybe she was just unhappy about it. She didn't looked exactly thrilled. And what was it that may not even—what? It was the last thing she'd said before she'd run out, and it was playing on his mind.

May not even be his?

He found bowls, glasses, forks, and headed back, setting the food and water down on the coffee table.

'Come on. Try it, please. Just a little.'

She tasted it suspiciously, refilled the fork and took another cautious mouthful, then another, and he felt a wash of relief.

He picked up his own fork and joined her, but the unanswered question was still there and he had to force himself to eat.

'Better?'

She was, surprisingly. At least the nausea was. The humiliation was another matter. 'Yes. Thank you. And I'm so sorry about the restaurant.'

'No, I'm sorry—'

'Why? You didn't know. I should have thought about it, suggested somewhere else. Here, maybe.'

'Well, we're here now, and we have a baby

to talk about. I'm still trying to get my head around that and I guess you are, too. Unless it's not mine?'

She stared at him, horrified that he could think that. 'Of course it's yours!'

'Is it? Because in the restaurant you said, "it may not even—" and then you broke off. What was it, Alice? May not even be mine? Is that what you were going to say?'

'No. Not that. It can only be yours, Marco. There hasn't been anyone else for years. Please believe me. I would never do that to you—to anyone.'

His eyes searched hers, and then he nodded slowly, just once, and she looked away, the tenderness in his eyes unnerving because whatever happened, whatever he said next, she was sure it would just be out of guilt and pity and she didn't want that, so she cut him off before he could start.

'I was going to say it may not even happen. It's very early days, I could lose it.'

A tiny frown flitted through his eyes. 'That's not likely. Many more pregnancies end in a baby than a miscarriage.'

Not necessarily in her case. But she wasn't ready to tell him anything so personal about herself. Not now. Maybe never, because she'd seen what that did to a relationship and she never wanted to see that expression on anyone's face again.

Disgust. Revulsion. And a rapid retraction of his proposal. And she hadn't dated anyone since—

'Alice?'

No. She wouldn't tell him. She sucked in a breath and met his eyes. 'Sorry. I'm just a pessimist. I can't believe it's happened. I never thought I'd ever be pregnant, especially not right after landing the job of my dreams, so I know it seems wrong but you'll have to forgive me for not being ecstatic about it. To be honest, I have no idea how I feel. I'm still getting over the shock.'

He gave a soft laugh. 'It wasn't exactly in my plans, either, but a baby's a baby, Alice. They're pretty harmless. I should know, I'm the oldest of eight, and I spent half my childhood changing nappies and pushing prams around the vineyards with a trail of small people following after me. There were times when I felt like a cross between the Pied Piper and Mary Poppins.'

That made her smile. 'I didn't realise you had such a large family. You've never talked about them before.'

'I don't. I love them, of course I do, but I don't see them very often. I disappointed them a long time ago—I was engaged to a lovely girl from a good family, and I couldn't give her what she needed, which was to stay at home near her family and have babies, rather than follow me around from one strange place to another while I did my rotations in England, so I ended it for both our sakes because I felt we were in love with the idea rather than each other. And then my family accused me of leading her on and breaking her heart because I'd been so selfish and uncaring and put myself first as usual, so I don't go back unless I have to. And I have to, in three weeks, because my little sister's getting married and I need to be there.'

'That's the long weekend you booked off?'

'Yes.' He was looking at her thoughtfully suddenly, and then he said, 'I told them I'd be bringing someone, mostly to defuse my mother's matchmaking efforts because despite the fiasco she *still* wants to see me married to someone she considers suitable, and a wedding is the perfect matchmaking opportunity, so I need a plus one or she'll be a nightmare. Why don't you come with me? It'll be fun.'

That shocked her. 'To your sister's wedding? I don't know any of them.'

'I know, but you need to, because they'll be a part of our child's life—'

'Why? And there *is* no child yet.'

He frowned. 'Why? Because they're my *fam-*

ily, Alice, and they'll want to be part of their grandchild's life.'

'Marco, they haven't *got* a grandchild yet! There's nothing to tell them. They don't need to know about the baby. Not for ages, maybe never if it goes wrong—'

'No, they don't. I agree. At this stage I'd rather they didn't. But it might help you get to know more about me if you met them, and anyway it's beautiful there. It'll be cool, but it's the end of the olive harvest and it'll be a huge celebration. My parents do seriously good weddings. And it'll give us time away from work to get to know each other. And whatever happens between us I think that's important, if we're having a child together.'

Having a child together? That sounded weird. So out of left field that she could hardly get her head round it.

'Can I think about it? This is all a bit sudden.'

'Yes, of course. If you decide not to come, I can always make an excuse. So—that's my family. What about yours?'

She relaxed a fraction. 'Oh, I have three brothers. I'm number three in the family, but we're all close together in age and we love each other to bits. One's a doctor, one's a vet, the other one a dentist. We're pretty competitive.'

'Are you winning?'

She laughed. 'Sort of. The vet and the dentist have their own practices, but the doctor's a mere specialist registrar at the moment, so, yes, I'm winning as far as the doctors go but I would say we're pretty equal. Except they're all married with children, but at least it takes the heat off me,' she said rashly without filtering her words, but he pounced on it.

'Why aren't you married?'

She blinked. 'Why aren't you?'

'Because it's not on my agenda, which I think was part of the reason it went wrong before. I'd just qualified as a registrar and I had my paeds training to complete. I needed all my focus, needed to be able to follow my career wherever it took me, and to a certain extent that's still true.'

'So you understand, then, why I'm single.'

He smiled wryly. 'Yeah, I guess I do.' He got to his feet, picked up the plates and took them through to the kitchen. She could hear him rinsing them, loading them into the dishwasher, then the tap running again, and he was back.

'I should go. You need an early night, but I'll see you in the morning. Make sure you eat before you get up. Toast, crackers, slivers of apple—'

'Marco, I'll be fine,' she said without any confidence if today was anything to go by, and got to her feet. 'Look—I don't want this all round the hospital. You know how people love a good juicy story.'

'Don't worry, I won't talk about it. I don't talk about private stuff, not at work, and especially not this.'

No, he didn't. Tonight was the first time either of them had talked about their families, and it helped to explain a little of how at ease he was with the children.

He'd be a brilliant father—

'Goodnight, Alice,' he said softly, and bending down, he touched a gentle, tender kiss to her lips and let himself out.

A brilliant father, an amazing lover and a good husband. And she was getting horribly ahead of herself, and it was so unlikely to happen. Even if she got through the pregnancy without incident, which wasn't likely, she'd still have to tell him about her condition, and then she'd see *that look* on his face and it would tear her apart.

She switched off the lights and went up to bed.

CHAPTER TWO

'MORNING.'

Alice swallowed a wave of nausea and looked up from her desk.

'Do you *ever* knock?'

He went back out of the door, knocked, walked in again and smiled mischievously. 'Good morning. There, is that better?'

She put her pen down and leant back with a sigh, stifling the urge to smile. 'You're supposed to wait for an answer. I assume you want something? And shut the door, please.'

He peered closer, and frowned. 'Are you OK?'

'Yes, I'm fine,' she lied. 'Thank you for last night—for looking after me—I appreciated it, but I'm fine now. So, what did you want?'

He shrugged as if he didn't believe her, but he let it pass. 'Just an update for you. I've checked the post-ops from yesterday, spent a few minutes with Amil and his parents in PICU—the boy with Crohn's?'

'I do know who Amil is. How is he today?'

'OK. He's had a reasonable night, apparently, which is excellent news, and we should be able to move him out of there later onto a ward. Hopefully the surgery will have done the trick for now and once he's on the mend we can hand him over to gastroenterology and see if they can get him a bit more settled on a new drug regime. So, boss lady, what's on the agenda for today?'

She swallowed another wave of nausea and looked down at the file of notes on her desk.

'Daisy Lawrence. She was diagnosed with malrotation of the gut as a toddler because she was having lots of stomach cramps without any other symptoms, but it wasn't considered severe enough for surgery at the time and they adopted a watch and wait policy, but she's flared up again, they've got private medical insurance and they wanted a second opinion so they chose us.'

He perched on the corner of her desk beside her and studied the notes. 'So what are we doing? X-rays, MRI, CT?'

'I'm not sure. I think we'll start with a follow-through contrast scan to see what's going on in there, so I've booked that with the imaging suite for this morning, and we'll review the results and see where we go from there, but I think we need to go and meet them and examine her and talk it through.'

'Are they here?'

She shook her head. 'I don't believe so. They're not due until nine. I was just going through her notes again.'

'So—have you had breakfast?' he asked, and she swallowed again and shook her head.

'I couldn't—'

'Well, isn't it a good job you have me to feed you?' he said, passing her a small packet of salty wholewheat crackers.

She eyed them with suspicion. Food? Really—?

'Eat them,' he instructed gently, and she tore the bag open reluctantly and tried one.

Surprisingly edible. She had another.

'OK?'

She nodded. 'Yes—thanks.' She took a sip of water and had another one while he flicked through the notes.

'Apparently watermelon is good if you feel sick,' he told her without looking up. 'Just a little piece. I've put some in the fridge in the staffroom where you keep your lunch. And you need carbs.'

'I don't eat carbs.'

He looked up and met her eyes. 'I noticed. That's why you're feeling sick, because your blood sugar is low because you're on one of these crazy celebrity diets where your body's in a permanently ketogenic state. It's bad for you.'

'It isn't. A ketogenic diet means I maintain a healthy weight and keep my blood sugar and cholesterol under control,' she said, feeling a little flicker of panic because he was getting too close to the truth and she didn't want to tell him, or at least not yet.

'Why on earth do you need to do that? You're not overweight, you're under if anything, and you spend your free time in the gym.'

'How do you know that? You're never in there.'

'No. I don't do gyms, but our colleagues use them, and they talk.'

She hated the idea of people talking about her. Speculating?

'So I keep fit—and I'm not underweight, my BMI is nineteen point five.'

'That's borderline underweight.' He frowned, his voice softening. 'Alice, is food a problem for you? Do you have an eating disorder?'

She stared at him, stunned. 'No! Of course I don't have an eating disorder! I've told you, I'm just keeping healthy—'

'Then why don't you eat cake if it's someone's birthday? Why do you always say no to snacks and biscuits? They won't kill you occasionally if you make an exception to avoid hurting someone's feelings.'

She sighed and gave up. 'Because I have insulin resistance,' she said flatly, giving him a symptom rather than a diagnosis just to get him off her back, but she could see it wasn't working. He frowned, looked thoughtful and tipped his head on one side.

'I just don't buy it. The only way you have insulin resistance is if you're borderline diabetic and have metabolic syndrome, which you haven't because you're much too thin for that, or you've got a hormonal imbalance or something like PCOS…'

He trailed to a halt, frowned again and searched her face, and she could hear the cogs turning as the frown softened into concern.

'Is that it? Is that why you were so surprised that you were pregnant, because you have PCOS?'

'That's a bit of a quantum leap, isn't it, from insulin resistance to polycystic ovaries?' she said, flannelling furiously because she wasn't ready to have this conversation. Wouldn't *ever* be ready to have it—

'Not for a doctor. And I know I'm a paediatric surgeon, but I'm still a doctor and I haven't forgotten everything I learned in med school. So is this why you were surprised you're pregnant, and why you're so convinced you could lose the baby, because of the risk of high blood pressure, pre-eclampsia, gestational diabetes, miscarriage—is there anything else? I'm sure there must be other things you're torturing yourself with.'

'So what if I have got it?' she asked, suddenly sick of not telling him and wanting to get the revulsion over, but there was no revulsion, to her surprise. Instead he shrugged away from the desk, put his arms round her and hugged her, tutting softly.

'Oh, Alice. Is this why you're not married? Why you're so defensive? Because some idiot didn't want a wife who couldn't be sure of giving him children?'

She eased out of his arms, her emotions all over the place, and if she stayed there with her head against him, she'd lose it and blub all over him. 'No. I'm not married because he didn't want a wife who was fat and hairy and had more testosterone than he did.'

He sat back on the edge of the desk, his eyes wide. 'But that's not you! You're not fat, and I can't believe you ever were because you're far too well controlled. Besides, most people don't have all those symptoms, if any. It's rubbish.'

'You don't have to tell me that, I know, but he didn't and once he'd researched it—which he did there and then on his phone, the minute I told him—he didn't hang around long enough for me to put him right,' she said, grabbing her pager like a lifeline as it bleeped.

'Daisy's here,' she said, sliding her chair back, and she stood up, picked up the notes and headed for the door, pausing to look over her shoulder. 'Well, are you coming, or are you going to stay here all day making annoying comments and quizzing me about my medical history?'

He rolled his eyes. 'Yes, of course I'm coming.' He straightened up, grabbed the bag of savoury crackers and followed her.

Polycystic ovary syndrome.

He never would have guessed if he hadn't pushed her, but now so much of her defensive behaviour made sense, especially in the light of some ignorant—

His thoughts lapsed into Italian, because he had a better grasp of the language he'd need to sum up someone that ignorant and cruel. No matter. He, whoever he was, was in the past, and now was for them. He'd look after her, take care of her and the baby, go to all her antenatal appointments with her and support her in any way she'd let him.

Assuming she'd let him, which was a big assumption.

He fell into step beside her. 'So, how old is Daisy?'

'Four. She's seeing us first and then being admitted to the assessment unit until we have a better idea of what's going on, and if and when we'll need to operate. She's coming in without breakfast ready for the contrast scan, so I don't want to keep her hanging about long because it's a slow process and she'll be hungry.'

'OK, so we'll go from there. Do you want me in on the consult?'

She stopped and turned to face him. 'Yes, because if she needs surgery, I'll want you in on it, and you're good with the children. And besides, I value your opinion.'

He resisted the overwhelming urge to smirk, restricting himself to a slight smile and a tiny shake of the head. 'Did that nearly kill you?'

She looked away, but not before he saw her mouth twitch. 'Don't be ridiculous. Your ego's showing again.'

'Oh, dear. Me and my ego. We're always in trouble.'

He swiped his lanyard, held the door open for her and followed her through to the consulting room waiting area.

A couple were sitting there, a small girl with

long blonde hair cuddled on the woman's knee, and he thought they looked uncomfortable, strained. With worry?

'Mr and Mrs Lawrence?' Alice said. They got to their feet and she held out her hand to them. 'Welcome to Hope Hospital. I'm Alice Baxter, the senior gastro-intestinal surgeon, and this is my colleague Marco Ricci. And you must be Daisy,' she said, bobbing down to the child's level. 'Hi, Daisy. You can call me Alice, if you like.'

'I'm Olive, and this is Dan,' Mrs Lawrence said, and smiled down encouragingly at Daisy. 'Daisy, say hello.'

But Daisy had obviously had enough of doctors, and she turned her face into her mother and hid, so Alice straightened up and smiled at her parents. 'Shall we go on through to the consulting room and talk through what we're planning to do today? And if it's all right, I'd like us to have a look at Daisy.'

She ushered them into the room, and Marco scooped up Daisy's forgotten teddy and followed them into the very room where he'd accidentally got Alice pregnant just over five weeks ago.

Was that really all it was? Thirty-eight days?

Trying not to look at the couch, he let Alice do the talking, taking the opportunity to sit on the floor and prop his back against the wall. Daisy was looking withdrawn and wary, so he hid the teddy behind his back and brought it out in surprising places. Under his other arm, behind his legs, upside down and sideways, and all the time Daisy watched him, warily at first, and then with a glimmer of anticipation.

And then finally she giggled, and he felt as if the sun had come out.

'Does your teddy have a name?' he asked her softly, and she nodded and moved a little nearer him—but not too near.

'He's called Wuzzle.'

'Wuzzle? What a lovely name. Hello, Wuzzle. Nice to meet you. I'm Marco. So, Wuzzle, what can you tell me about Daisy?'

'She's my best friend,' he said, pretending to be a ventriloquist and making Daisy giggle again.

'And what else can you tell me, Wuzzle?'

'She's got a sore tummy.'

He put the teddy down and looked at Daisy. 'Is that right, Daisy? Do you have a sore tummy?'

Daisy nodded and sat down facing him. 'Sometimes, especially when I've had my dinner.'

'Oh, no. That's a pity. So do you just have a little bit of dinner then?' he asked, because she was a skinny, lanky little thing and it could have been because she'd had a growth spurt or because her appetite was off. Especially if she was afraid to eat. And she was pale and wan. Worryingly so.

She nodded. 'If I eat too much, my tummy hurts.'

'OK, Daisy, I have an idea. Will you let me and Alice try and find out what's wrong with your tummy?' he asked gently. 'Because we can't have you hurting, can we, when you eat?'

She shook her head. 'Wuzzle's tummy hurts, too.'

'Does it? Can you show me where?'

Daisy pressed her fingers gently onto Wuzzle's soft, furry body, around about what would be his epigastric region if he wasn't a teddy bear. 'Here,' she said, and pressed again to the right. 'And here.'

'Is that the same place as your tummy?'

She nodded, and snuggled Wuzzle tight against her chest.

'OK. Daisy, do you mind if I have a little feel of your tummy now? See if I can feel anything wrong? Would that be OK?'

She nodded again, her brown eyes soft and wounded, and he felt his heart wrench for her.

'Come on, then, poppet. Let's help you up onto the bed and I can have a look at both of you, OK?'

He stood up, pulled Daisy to her feet, handed Wuzzle to her and lifted them easily onto the couch. The couch where he and Alice had made not only love, but a baby. Amazing...

'Now, let's have a look at Wuzzle first, shall we?'

Alice's eyes strayed to him, to his gentle, careful hands examining first the teddy and then little Daisy, with just the same thoroughness and attention to detail he'd brought to their lovemaking right there on the edge of that couch.

Did he realise it was the same room?

'He's so good with her,' Olive said quietly, and she nodded.

'Yes, he is.' Good with everything...

She turned away from Marco and gave the Lawrences her undivided attention. 'Has anybody explained to you what malrotation of the gut is, exactly?'

Daisy's mother nodded. 'Something to do with the way she formed as an embryo, they said, and I've worried ever since that it was something I ate or did—'

'No. It was nothing you did. There's no evidence to suggest anything of the sort. What happens is that the cells that become the gut migrate up into the umbilical cord at about ten weeks of pregnancy, and then at around eleven weeks they migrate back down again, and coil into the area that becomes the abdomen. And sometimes, about once in every five hundred babies, they coil the wrong way, because our bodies aren't symmetrical inside.

'The liver is on the right, the spleen and pancreas and stomach on the left, and the small intestine starts at the bottom of the stomach and curls around past the liver, picking up the bile and pancreatic ducts, and then this great tangle of small intestine wriggles around inside and joins the large bowel down on the right, where we get appendicitis.

'In children with malrotation it coils the other way, so that join in the gut can end up near their stomach or even on the other side, so diagnosing appendicitis is difficult, and that's often when asymptomatic malrotation is diagnosed.

'The problem arises when the part that is trying to be the right way round gets twisted somehow in a bit of a conflict of interests with the other bit, and that twisting process can lead to what's known as a volvulus, which means the blood supply to that part is kinked and cut off by the twisting, and that's a life-threatening emergency.

'Daisy is *not* at that stage, but she may be approaching it, because she could have bands of fibrous tissue called Ladd's bands holding her intestines in the wrong place. That's what our tests today are going to look for, to find out exactly how her gut is coiled inside her, and where the pinch points or twists might lie so we can rearrange her gut to relieve that, if it's what's causing her pain. Does that make sense?'

They nodded, but she noticed they didn't offer each other any support or interact in any way, which seemed odd.

'Is there anything else we can tell you before we admit her and she goes down for her scan?'

They shook their heads, again not conferring.

'OK, that's good. Feel free to ask, though, at any time, because I know it's a lot to take in. So, Dr Marco, what's the verdict?' she asked lightly, turning to face the examination couch again. 'Do Daisy and Wuzzle need to have some pictures taken?'

He turned his head and smiled. 'Yes, I think they do. I think we need to find out why they've got tummy ache. So, Dr Alice, how are we going to take the pictures?'

'Well, Daisy, after you've been checked in by a nurse we'll take you downstairs, and a lady there will give you a special drink, and then we'll take pictures of the drink all through the morning as it moves through your tummy. It's called a follow-through contrast scan, and it's very good at showing us where things aren't working quite like they should be. Is that OK?'

'Will Wuzzle have some to drink, too?'

'I'm sure he can. Would you like strawberry, blackcurrant or chocolate flavour?'

Daisy tipped her head to one side and contorted her little face thoughtfully. 'Chocolate,' she said in the end, sounding a little bit triumphant as if she'd just made an important decision, and Alice stifled a smile.

'Chocolate it is, then,' she said, and on the way to the admissions unit she managed to get a few words with Marco.

'So?' she murmured softly, trying to concentrate on Daisy and not the warmth she could feel radiating from his body, the scent that was uniquely him.

'There's a firm mass in the upper right quadrant—it could be the start of a volvulus or simply the adhesions restraining the midgut. If her gut's only just beginning to twist it could explain why it's been intermittent, but I don't think she's far off having a full-on volvulus, so I think we may need to operate tomorrow, if not today. Her abdomen was a little tense and it's definitely sore.'

'And Wuzzle?'

He smiled, his eyes softening and threatening to melt her insides. 'I think Wuzzle might need to have a few stitches and a little plaster on his tummy,' he said in a low murmur, and Alice felt the warm drift of his breath against her skin and a ripple of need went through her. It would be so easy to lean against him, just to feel that warmth, that strength, that solid wall of muscle.

She moved away a fraction and smiled up at him.

'That sounds like your department,' she murmured, and he chuckled softly, sending that enticing drift of air over her again, and she took herself out of range for the sake of her sanity.

He paused as Alice opened the door to the admissions unit and ushered the Lawrences through, and Daisy turned and looked at him, her little face worried.

'Aren't you coming with me?' she asked him, her chin wobbling, so he walked back towards her and crouched down.

'I can't. I have to go and see a little boy who had an operation yesterday and make sure he's comfy and happy and that everything's going well, but then I'll come back and see you if you like.'

'Promise?'

He glanced up at Alice, and she nodded.

'Yes. I promise. Alice will ask them to tell

me when you're ready, and I'll go downstairs with you when you have the pictures taken of your tummy, but Mummy and Daddy will be there, too. Nobody's going to leave you alone, poppet. It's OK.'

She nodded, then gave him a little hug, Wuzzle brushing up against his face. 'OK,' she said, and he eased away and stood up, a lump in his throat for some reason.

'I'll be as quick as I can,' he promised, and he waved goodbye to Daisy and left them to go up and check on Amil, the child with Crohn's in PICU.

Evie, the ICU receptionist, resident baby-cuddler and organiser of miracles, including the opening gala, was at her post in the reception area outside the unit, and she looked up and smiled at him and he paused, glad to see her there because, if the hospital grapevine was correct, she and Ryan Walker had just got engaged after a whirlwind romance.

He leant on the desk and grinned at her. 'Hi, Evie. I gather congratulations are in order. That's fabulous news.'

Evie smiled with every part of her face. 'It is, isn't it? And Ryan and I are hoping to adopt baby Grace.'

'Really? Oh, that's amazing. How is she?'

'Oh, she's wonderful—she's doing so well I

can't believe she's the same tiny newborn we found by the bins. She's so strong now, I'm really proud of her. It's all down to Ryan's surgery on her poor little heart, of course—'

'That's not what I've heard, I reckon it was all the love you gave her,' he said with a smile. He hesitated, then leant closer. 'Have you seen the Khans today? They've found Amil's illness very distressing. Can you keep an eye on them? They're struggling a bit.'

'Of course. I was talking to them earlier. They seem better today. Yesterday was hard for them.'

'I'm sure. I'm just going to see him now. Thanks, Evie.'

Amil was doing well, to Marco's relief.

He was propped up slightly and seemed to be pain-free, thanks to the epidural, and his notes showed a steady heart rate and blood pressure.

His mother was sitting with him, reading him a story, and although the strain still showed in her face, her eyes were more relaxed and she smiled up at him.

'How's it going?' he asked, and the boy's eyes filled.

'It doesn't hurt. That's the first time in so long.'

Courtesy of the epidural. 'Good. That's what

we want. Now we just need to give your gut time to mend, and then we can start you on food and see how that goes, but you're getting food through your drip in your arm, so your body's getting all the food and water it needs, which means there's no hurry. Mind if I have a look at your tummy?'

'No.'

There was no bleeding under the transparent dressing, and his wound looked good. Neat sutures, so with luck he'd heal with hardly any scarring. He felt a flicker of satisfaction and covered Amil up again.

'OK, I'm happy. If you carry on like this, we should be able to move you down to HDU on the ward soon. Anything either of you want to ask me?'

They both shook their heads, so he left them to it and went back out into Reception.

'How is he?' Evie asked.

'He's doing well, and you're right, his mum looks much happier. So, what are you up to now? I'm sure Theo's got you planning something else amazing after the success of the gala.'

'Oh, all sorts of things. I had an idea, though. I was watching something about PAT dogs— Pets As Therapy?—and I suggested to Theo that maybe we could introduce it here, give it a try and see if the children benefit. It sounds such an amazing idea.'

'It is. I know a lady with a PAT dog. Her name's Alana, and she's got a soppy labradoodle—a Labrador poodle cross—called Doodle. He's the gentlest dog I've ever met, and he's just lovely and he smiles with his whole face. I could ask her if she'd be interested in coming here so we could trial the idea. I can think of lots of children who'd benefit from an ice breaker like that, and she's had people who tell the dog things they'd never tell a person. It can be a way of helping them to acknowledge their fears, and she's had great success with him, which doesn't surprise me, he just loves everyone unconditionally. He's gorgeous. Do you want me to talk to Theo before I speak to her, or will you?'

'Oh, I can if you like. I've got a meeting with him this afternoon to discuss the arrangements for Halloween and the Guy Fawkes firework display, so I could tack it onto that, if you don't mind? I'm sure he'll say yes.'

Marco nodded. 'That would be great. Let me know what he says, and then if he gives us the go-ahead, I'll talk to Alana. Right, I have to go. Daisy and Wuzzle are having a follow-through contrast scan and Daisy says they need me.'

Evie's lips twitched. 'Wuzzle?'

'Her teddy.' He pulled a sad face. 'He might

need stitches too. They may be up here, possibly today, maybe tomorrow. I'll let you know. You may have to look after Wuzzle.'

She smiled. 'I'm sure I can manage that.'

His pager bleeped, and he glanced at it. 'OK, Daisy's ready. I need to go. Let me know how it goes with Theo.'

The follow-through scan showed several areas that were minor pinch points, and one loop that was clearly a borderline volvulus. Anything could tip it over the edge and cut off the circulation, and there were Ladd's bands, which were holding the gut in the wrong position and making it all much worse. And Alice was worried.

'I think you're right. I think we need to operate as soon as we can, preferably today. She's been starved, she's not critical, she's reasonably well. I don't want to wait for this to turn into a crisis in the middle of the night so we need to get her on a drip, drain her gut and upper bowel with a nasogastric tube and then operate as soon as she's ready.'

'Are you OK with that?' Marco asked her, his voice low.

'Of course I am. Why not?'

He shrugged, but his concern was written all over his face, and she resisted the urge to give in and let him look after her, because she was only pregnant, for goodness' sake, not ill! But she did need to eat, and soon, or she would be.

'Can we take this conversation to the cafeteria? I didn't get round to making lunch today.'

'Of course. And then you need a nap while I talk to them and prep Daisy for the op.'

'I can't nap in the middle of the day!' she protested, but he just raised an eyebrow, opened the door of her office for her and fell in beside her.

'So, what are you going to eat, if you can't eat carbs?'

'I don't know. I'll see what they've got. Something high calorie and not too smelly, like avocado or cold salmon or something harmless.'

'Hmm. I tell you what. We'll get Daisy sorted, and then tomorrow night I'm cooking you dinner.'

She felt a flicker of panic. 'No, Marco. You don't know what makes me feel queasy, you don't know what I can eat—'

'Alice, I'm not stupid. Trust me.'

Could she? She wanted to, because the thought of prepping food made her stomach churn, but she had to eat.

And judging by the options available in the cafeteria, that could be awkward. She helped herself from the salad bar, added a portion of cold salmon and a cup of mint tea and picked her way through it while Marco ate his way steadily through a mountain of food.

Oddly, it didn't affect her, mostly because he'd chosen things that didn't smell. Because of her?

'Are you OK with what I'm eating?'

'Yes, I'm fine, but I'm guessing it wasn't your first choice.'

His mouth twitched. 'Don't worry about me. So, how are you going to fit this nap in?'

She rolled her eyes and put down her fork. 'Marco, I'm a busy doctor. I don't have time for a little nap in the middle of the day! I have too much to do.'

'So delegate to me. I can talk to parents, examine patients, write letters—even if you sign them. I can review results, order tests—use me, Alice. Make time for yourself, even if it's just half an hour at lunchtime after you eat. Please.'

She closed her eyes, just the thought of a nap so appealing she could have cried. 'Marco, really, I'll be fine. I don't need a nap, and I don't need you clucking over me like a mother hen. I want to talk about Daisy and her management.'

He shrugged, stuffed another forkful of food into his mouth and gestured to her to go on. Nothing said 'Suit yourself' louder than that did, and she realised that getting him to back down was going to be a fight she'd probably lose.

But nevertheless, the fact that he so obviously cared and wanted to look after her left a warm feeling inside. A feeling she wasn't sure she'd ever felt before, and it nearly made her cry…

CHAPTER THREE

SHE WENT WITH Marco to see Daisy, and while he was busy ordering blood tests and discussing her transfer to the surgical unit with the ward staff in the admissions unit, Alice took Daisy's mother into the office to talk to her.

Her father was nowhere to be seen, and Alice asked Olive if she wanted to contact him so they could discuss the results and what they were going to do for Daisy together, but she gave an awkward smile and shook her head.

'No, it's OK, Dan's busy, he had things to get on with,' she said, and it sounded as if she was being evasive.

'We can wait for him if you like?' she offered, but again Olive shook her head.

'We've got our own business and—well, it takes a lot of time, especially since he's on his own now. We worked together building the business for over ten years before Daisy came along, and ever since it's been—I don't know. Because of her illness I haven't felt happy leaving her with anyone so I don't help him any longer and to be honest it's probably easier that way. He can't handle Daisy being ill, being in pain, so he leaves her to me largely. It doesn't mean he doesn't love her, but we just tend to do our own thing now.'

That was an unexpected outpouring of honesty, and Alice reached out and touched her hand. 'I'm sorry, I didn't realise that. Well, I'm sure you can pass on anything I tell you, and if he wants to talk to me I'll be more than happy to go through it again. I'm always here for you both, so's Marco.' She sat back and pulled up Daisy's scan results on the tablet. 'So, this is what we found out this morning.'

She showed Olive the scan results, explained what they were going to do and how it would help Daisy, and then discussed the method they'd use to operate.

'Ideally we'd like to do it with keyhole surgery, and we'll remove the appendix because it's in the wrong place and that could make it hard to diagnose appendicitis.'

'Is she likely to get it?'

Alice shook her head. 'No more likely than anyone else, but if she gets abdominal pain in the future it eliminates it as a possibility. I have to warn you, though, that we may need to revert to open surgery if we can't get what we consider to be proper and sufficient access to the bits we're worried about.'

'So who's going to operate?'

'Both of us—me and Marco.'

'Is he good?'

She thought of their banter over Amil's sutures, and smiled. 'Yes. He's very good. Better than that, actually. He's excellent, and I trust him absolutely.'

Olive's face crumpled slightly. 'I can't believe she needs an operation, but she's been getting more and more uncomfortable and miserable, and sometimes she wakes up in the night crying with the pain. Dan can't cope with it, he just gets up and goes to the office and leaves me with her, as if I can cope with it any better, but I'm her mother, I can't walk out when she hurts just because it's too upsetting—'

She broke down in tears, worn out with the strain of it as so many parents were, but she was coping alone without her husband's support, and Alice put an arm round her and comforted her while she cried.

How could Dan have abandoned her to deal with this alone? Busy or not, she couldn't imagine Marco walking out and leaving his child, but then Olive hadn't probably expected that, either, and you couldn't know until you were tested how you'd behave. Still, ten years together before Daisy came along was surely long enough to know each other—unless it hadn't been a surprise? Maybe Dan had always avoided anything difficult?

She'd only known Marco a few months but she thought she knew him better than that. Was she deluding herself? After all, what did she really know of him outside work? Nothing. Well, a little about his family now, but not much. Maybe he'd behave just like Dan? Except he'd made it perfectly clear the moment she'd told him she was having a baby that he was in it for the long haul, so he clearly wasn't one to avoid tackling difficult issues.

Although the chronic illness of a much-loved child would be a challenge to anyone, and it was easy to make assumptions about how he'd behave. She wasn't even sure what she'd be like if Daisy was hers.

Agonised by every pang the child had, she realised. And not all parents had a support network. Theo Hawkwood, their own CEO and a former paediatric surgeon, was facing this alone with Ivy, his little daughter, and without the help of his beloved late wife, Hope. Ivy had been unwell for a few weeks now, with progressive pain and weakness in her legs, and so far, despite the cumulative brains of the highly talented, hand-picked staff within Theo's own Hope Hospital, nobody seemed to be able to work out what was wrong with her, hence waiting for the world-renowned American diagnostician Madison Archer to arrive, and you could tell he was worried, just like any other parent.

Just like Olive—and probably, although he wasn't here to show it, her husband Dan. Worried, and coping the only way they knew how.

The tears had subsided now, and Olive straightened up and blew her nose.

'I'm sorry—I don't know what came over me.'

'I do, and it's a perfectly normal reaction. Why don't you go and get a cup of tea or coffee and have a little break, and Marco and I will get the consent forms ready and everything lined up so we can operate as soon as Daisy's been prepped for surgery. It'll be a few hours yet, probably not until four, but we don't really want to leave her overnight because we could end up having to do it as an emergency on a much sicker little girl, and nobody wants that.'

'No, of course not. I'll go and get a coffee and ring Dan and talk to him, get him to come back.'

'OK. If you want to talk to me again, just ask anyone to page me and they can get hold of me. And please don't worry, Olive. We're here for you and Dan, as well as Daisy.'

Olive nodded and dredged up a wobbly smile. 'Thank you.'

'My pleasure.'

She showed Olive out of her office, went back to the admissions unit and found Marco.

'Have you had that nap yet?' he asked, and she rolled her eyes.

'No, I haven't. I've been talking to Olive Lawrence. She's going to get hold of her husband and talk to him.' She lowered her voice. 'He doesn't do Daisy's sickness, apparently. Can't cope with it.'

Marco scowled and made a disgusted noise, and she didn't need a psychology degree to work out what he was thinking.

'So, what's the plan?' he asked. 'Are we going ahead?'

'I think so. I sent her off to get a coffee, and when she comes back we'll get the NG tube in and the drip up.'

'I've done the drip,' he said. 'She was in pain again, so I've written her up for some IV pain relief. I think we need to get on with it before this escalates.'

She nodded. 'OK. I can send someone down to find her mother. She'll be in the café in the main reception area, trying to get hold of Dan. She needs to be here for the NG tube. It's bound to make Daisy gag and she'll need her mummy to hold her hand while it's done.'

'I agree. Everything's ready when you are. Just give me a call when you've seen the parents and I'll come straight back. I want to be there for her when they do the tube.'

'Where are you going?'

'Just to check on Amil again, and I've got a couple of discharge letters to write and I need to chase up Daisy's bloods. I'll be in your office.'

'OK.'

Why on earth had he said he wanted to be there?

It wasn't necessary, the nurses knew exactly what they were doing and they were brilliant at putting children at their ease, but Daisy had latched onto him after the game with Wuzzle and he didn't want anything getting in the way of her going into Theatre as soon as possible.

Which was how he ended up volunteering to have an NG tube inserted, to show a frightened little girl that it was harmless.

She was on the general surgical ward now, settled into her new bed, and he found himself parked in the chair beside the bed, subjecting himself to having a tube passed up his nose and down into his stomach.

Why had he suggested it?

'OK, Marco?'

He summoned up a grin. 'Yeah, go ahead, I'm fine.'

'Here, have Wuzzle,' Daisy said, holding him out. 'He wants to cuddle you.'

'Thank you, Daisy.'

He took the little bear, snuggled him against his chest and then he winked at Daisy, picked up the paper cup of water with a straw in it and waited while the nurse slid the nasogastric tube carefully up his nose. It made his eye stream— just the one, on the side of the tube—and then it hit the back of his throat and made him gag slightly, so he took a suck of the water to stifle his gag reflex and help him swallow it down, his eyes still on Daisy.

He gave her another wink as the nurse finished, then slowly pulled it out himself, wiped his nose and grinned at Daisy. 'See? Easy. What's that, Wuzzle?' He held the bear to his ear, nodded and then said, 'Wuzzle says it's OK and not to worry, he'll cuddle you, too.'

She didn't look convinced. 'Did it hurt?'

'No. It tickles. That's why I coughed. If you drink the water, it helps a lot. Then you just swallow and down it goes, easy-peasy. It feels a bit funny but it's OK.'

'Will you put it in?' she asked, and he nodded and handed Wuzzle back to her.

'Sure, if you want me to.'

'I do.'

'OK. Mum, if you sit her on your lap and hold her hand, that would be good. So, first I have to measure it, from the tip of your nose to your ear, and then down to your tummy—like that, and then I mark it so I know how far it has to go, because everybody's different and my tube was much longer and fatter because I'm bigger than you. So, there, it's marked, and now I just have to dip the end of the tube into this slippery stuff to help it slide down nice and easily, and in it goes. OK, Daisy? You're doing really well. Nice and still for me—good girl! Have a little drink, that's it, and swallow—and that's lovely. Keep drinking—good girl! It's in! There.'

He grinned at Daisy and gave her a high five while the nurse taped the tube to her cheek, tucked it behind her ear and attached a large syringe to the port to withdraw her stomach contents before she taped it to Daisy's gown so it didn't move.

Marco turned round to talk to Alice, and found she'd gone.

Because watching had triggered her gag reflex? Very likely. How he'd stifled his he had no idea, but it had done the trick and Daisy was all tubed up and ready to go.

'You're a brave girl, Daisy. Well done,' he said gently, and her mother's eyes filled.

'Thank you. Thank you so much for doing that.'

'My pleasure.' Well, that was a lie, but, hey. 'I'll bring you the consent form for the surgery, and then I'll talk you and Daisy through it.'

'Alice tells me you'll both be in Theatre. She speaks very highly of you.'

He chuckled. 'You're not supposed to tell me that. She say's my ego's big enough for both of us.'

Olive smiled sadly. 'I don't think you've got an ego, Marco. I think you're amazing. Thank you.'

'It's all part of the job,' he said softly, and went to get the forms.

It was a long operation, and for a while Alice wasn't sure they'd be able to recoil the gut into a safe position without open surgery.

'It doesn't want to go,' she said, and Marco took the other instruments and moved the bowel carefully to one side.

'There's another adhesion. Can you reach it?'

And then it moved, slowly but surely, allowing them to work the coils into a better position. The section of bowel that had been slightly darker instantly pinked up, and she sighed with relief.

'Brilliant. Well done.'

'So much praise today. My head's going to fall off under its own weight at this rate.'

'Praise?'

'Yes, from Olive, and from you, apparently,' he said, carefully manoeuvring the last coil into position. 'She said you spoke highly of me. That was after you bolted.'

She could feel herself colouring. 'Sorry. I had to.'

'I guessed that. I could have done with bolting, too. I don't know why I volunteered.'

'Because you're a nice man,' she said, realising it was true. There weren't many people who'd do that, they'd leave it to the nurses to talk the children round, and if necessary do it with sedation. Not Marco. Oh, no. He had to have it done to show her how easy it was. Except it wasn't, because however you looked at it, it was unpleasant.

'Did Dan show up in the end?'

'No,' he said, and his eyes over the mask were disapproving.

'Not everyone can cope with it, Marco.'

'I know that, and I don't know that I could. I just know you try. You do it even if it hurts you, because if it hurts you and scares you, you can be sure it hurts and scares the child far more. You can't escape that by running away. OK, I think we're done. Are you happy?'

'For now,' she said. 'We might need to go back in if it doesn't resolve or if it moves again, but I think we've done all we can for now and I don't want to open her up and slow her recovery unnecessarily.'

'No, I agree. I'll close, you go and talk to Olive and then go home. It's nearly eight and I bet you haven't eaten.'

'I have. I had something earlier, but I've got admin to do. Come and find me when you're done.'

'OK.'

She went out, and to her surprise found Dan there with Olive. They both leapt to their feet as she emerged, and she smiled at them encouragingly.

'She's fine, we've sorted it out, her bowel is looking much happier now and we managed to do it without open surgery, so assuming it all settles down in the next day or two and we don't have to go back in, her recovery time should be much quicker. Marco's just closing, then they'll take her through to Recovery and then back to the ward. She'll be in the high dependency unit on the ward, but don't be alarmed. It's just because they'll be checking on her every half hour or so and it keeps the rest of the ward quieter for the children who need less intervention in the night.'

'Oh. That makes sense. Thank you so much.'

'Yes, thank you,' Dan chipped in, looking uncomfortable. 'I'm sorry I wasn't here earlier, I find it really hard to see her like that.'

'You don't need to apologise to me,' she said gently. 'It is hard and not everyone can do it, but Daisy could do with all the support she can get, and so could both of you.'

He nodded, but he didn't look convinced, just worried, stressed and unsupported, like Olive.

Was their marriage under strain because of Daisy's condition? It sounded like it.

'Look, she'll be a while yet. Why don't you go down to the cafeteria and get yourselves something to eat and drink? It could be a long night if you're going to sit up with her, although she'll be sedated and have pain relief so you could go back to your family suite after you've seen her, if you'd rather, and we'll contact you if we need you. But in the meantime take advantage of the fact that you can't do anything else and look after yourselves, OK? Because it's tough being the parents of a sick child, and you need to cut yourselves some slack.'

They nodded, and she walked back across the link to the central building where her office was, shut the door and sat down with a tired sigh.

She was exhausted.

The pregnancy? It was ridiculous, in gestational terms she was only seven and a half weeks pregnant. How could she be so tired? Maybe Marco was right, maybe she needed a few more carbs in her diet. Or a nap, but that was never going to happen. She pulled open the drawer, took out the last of the little wholewheat crackers he'd given her this morning and ate a couple, then leant back and shut her eyes.

Just for a moment…

She was asleep.

He watched her for a moment, surprised by the surge of tenderness and—no, surely not love. He didn't know her well enough to love her. But he suddenly realised he wanted to, to know her well enough, and to love her. Was it possible? Would she let him get that close, let him into her heart? And could he let her into his? Did he want to?

Yes—and that surprised him. He'd broken up with Francesca because he'd known in his heart of hearts he didn't love her enough, any more than she loved him, and since the ensuing emotional fallout with his family he'd always kept his emotional distance from the women in his life, wary of causing any more heartache and so held something back, but suddenly—because of the baby she was carrying?—he wanted a much greater closeness with Alice, a deeper intimacy, an intimacy of their hearts and minds, not just their bodies.

The physical side he could have with anyone, although probably not as good as it had been with Alice, but to have that special closeness, that meeting of souls bonded together by their love for each other and their child—could he have that with Alice? Would she let him that close to her?

Even the thought of it put a lump in his throat, a tight knot of longing in his chest, and he took a long, slow breath in and blew it out, calming his body, slowing his heart. There was no hurry, no urgency. He'd work at it slowly, take it day by day, and prove to her that she could trust him. And maybe then...

He crossed to her side, laid his hand gently on her shoulder and shook it slightly.

'Alice? Alice, wake up,' he murmured.

She straightened, sucking in a breath and blinking at him.

'Oh—sorry. I must have dozed off. What's the time?'

'Half past nine.'

'Really? Gosh. How's Daisy?'

'She's fine, so's Amil. They're both settled for the night, everyone else is fine so you don't need to worry. Go home, Alice. You're exhausted, and you need your sleep.'

'I can't go home. Someone needs to be here.'

'Yes—me. I've told Daisy's parents I'll be here all night in an on-call room, so you don't need to do anything.'

'But what if she has to go back into Theatre?'

'I'll call you, but she won't. She's fine, she's looking good. She's nice and drowsy and she's comfortable, and she doesn't need you, and she doesn't need me, so go home now and get some decent rest, and I'll see you in the morning, OK?'

She nodded tiredly, stretched, yawned and got to her feet, reaching for her coat.

'Are you sure you don't need me?'

That nearly made him laugh. Need her? He'd always needed her. Ever since he'd met her he'd needed her, and since the gala it had been far worse, tormenting him day and night. Once had been nothing like enough, but that wasn't what she meant, so he stuck to the script.

'No, I don't need you,' he said firmly. 'I can cope with a sleeping child. It's not like there aren't dozens of staff here to help me. Go on. Shoo.'

She nodded, walked over to him and went up on tiptoe and kissed his cheek.

'Thank you,' she murmured, and then left the room.

He closed his eyes, ran the last twenty-four hours through his mind and shook his head.

It seemed incredible, but it was only this time yesterday that he'd found out he was going to be a father, and it had changed his life.

It had been a long, long day. Time for one last check of his little charges, and then bed. And hopefully, tonight, he'd sleep.

'Don't forget I'm cooking for you tonight.'

Alice tilted her head and frowned at him. 'You are? When did I say yes to that?'

He smiled. 'Yesterday.'

'I didn't say yes!'

He smiled again. 'Not in so many words, but I took it as read.'

'Well, you don't need to be so presumptuous. I might have plans.'

'Do you have plans?'

Damn. She couldn't lie to him. 'No. I don't have plans.'

His mouth twitched but he managed not to laugh out loud at her, to her relief. 'Well, you do now. I've got my car here. We'll go when we finish. Oh, and I got you these.'

He handed her a small packet of pills.

'Folic acid?' She felt a twinge of worry, and

he must have read her mind because he shook his head.

'You'll be fine. You have a very good diet full of folic acid, if the fridge here is anything to go by. Lots of dark leafy greens, any carbs I've ever seen you eat have been wholegrains—really, Alice, you'll be fine, but you should be taking them, just to be sure. And if you take multivitamins, nothing with vitamin A. Too much—'

'Is potentially harmful. I know.' She frowned down at them, glanced back up at him and smiled ruefully. 'Thank you, Marco. It was very thoughtful of you.' Like everything he was doing for her now.

He grunted. 'Don't thank me. It's my baby, too.'

As if she could forget. And that's what this was all about, of course. Making sure the baby was OK. The fact that he had to take care of her to ensure its safety was just a by-product, and she swallowed down the little pang of regret that it wasn't just for her. Or at least she didn't think so. 'How are Daisy and Amil?' she asked, getting back onto safer ground.

'Doing well. Daisy was a bit sore this morning so I upped her pain relief, Amil is making very good progress. I think we can discharge Tyler and Abbie today, too. Oh, and Ivy Hawkwood's not doing so well. I saw Evie up at

PICU—we were talking about introducing a PAT dog to see how the children got on with it, and she was going to discuss it with Theo but apparently he had to cut their meeting short and go home. I think he's possibly talking about admitting her for further tests.'

'Oh, no. I wonder what's wrong with her? Have they ruled out a brain or spinal tumour?'

'I don't know what they've done, but he must be worried sick. Whatever it is it seems to come and go so a tumour's unlikely, but she's only five. That's very young for something like MS but from what Evie said the symptoms seem to fit.'

'Gosh. Poor little Ivy. Oh, Marco, I hope it's nothing awful. He's lost his wife. He doesn't need to lose his daughter. That would be too sad.'

'Tell me about it. So—have you had breakfast?'

She laughed and shook her head slowly. 'You don't give up, do you? Yes, I've had breakfast. I had scrambled eggs on wilted spinach. And I've brought some lunch and other snacks. I seem to be able to eat avocado and just about anything with salt on it, for some reason. And, yes, I'm resisting the urge to overdo the salt in case I get high blood pressure, before you ask. Right, shall we do some work or is there anything else you need to nag me about before we start?'

He bit his lips, his eyes sparkling with laughter, and she had the sudden and almost irresistible urge to kiss him.

She checked on Daisy herself, and found her snuggled up to Wuzzle, her mother by her side as usual.

'Hello, Daisy,' she said softly, sending a smile to Olive. 'How are you feeling today?'

'A bit sore, but so is Wuzzle and Marco says he'll get better soon, too. See.'

She held the teddy out, and Alice saw four tiny, bright blue sutures scattered around his abdomen, in just the same place as Daisy's. Marco again, going the extra mile to comfort a child.

'Marco says he can have his stitches out tomorrow, but I might have to wait a little longer.'

'I think teddies get better quicker,' Alice said, not sure about going along with this fiction but backing Marco regardless, because it seemed to make Daisy happy and that was all that mattered.

'Can I have a look at your tummy, too?' she asked, and Daisy lifted her arms up so Alice could turn back the covers. Perfect little sutures, beautifully done—of course—but her abdomen seemed a little tense and that worried Alice.

'Does this hurt?' she asked, pressing gently and then letting go suddenly, and she got her answer in a flicker of pain across Daisy's little face.

'A bit,' she said bravely.

Alice covered her again, scanned the chart at the foot of the bed and frowned. She seemed to be on quite a lot of pain relief, and it wasn't working. Would they need to go in again?

'Is something wrong?' Olive asked, and Alice shook her head.

'No, I don't think so. Daisy, may I borrow Mummy for a minute? I want to ask her a few things.'

'OK,' she said, and Alice wasn't sure if it was the light or if she was looking slightly flushed.

They moved away from the bed, and Olive immediately asked again if something was wrong.

'It could be. Has she eaten anything yet?'

Olive shook her head. 'No. She tried but she retched. All she's had is a little water and she didn't really want that.'

'OK. Well, her abdomen's tense, and she's got what we call rebound tenderness, a pain brought on when you release the pressure suddenly. That could indicate peritonitis or a twisted bowel. Either would explain why she can't eat. I want to run a few more tests, and depending on what we find we may have to take her back to Theatre because there may be something else going on that we missed.'

Olive's face crumpled, and Alice led her round the corner out of Daisy's line of sight.

'It's just a possibility at this stage, and it was always a possibility. We hoped we wouldn't have to take her back in, and maybe we won't, but in the meantime why don't you go and get a coffee and we can keep her company and set up the tests. I want some more bloods and another X-ray before we make a decision.'

Olive nodded and went back to Daisy to pick up her bag and explain where she was going, and Alice paged Marco.

She was requesting the tests when he appeared at her side and she filled him in.

'Rebound tenderness? That's new, she didn't have it earlier.'

'It's only slight—but she's on quite a bit of pain relief.'

'I know. How are her obs?'

'OK, stable. No raised temperature, but she's looking a little flushed.'

'She looked pale as I walked past an hour ago. She seemed to be asleep. What are you thinking?'

'Peritonitis or volvulus. According to Olive she's only had drinks, and when they tried to get her to eat something for breakfast she retched. I think we're going to have to go back in.'

He swore softly in Italian, then sighed. 'I didn't want to do this.'

'Neither did I. Let's run the tests and see. Another contrast scan should give us the answer.'

It did. For some reason, or no reason at all, the gut had twisted on itself and she had a volvulus, cutting off the blood supply to almost all her midgut.

They took her straight to Theatre, made a midline incision and Alice reached in, carefully eased the gut out and turned the tangled mass back anticlockwise to free it. Immediately the little coils began to pink up, but not all of it seemed to be free to move.

'There must be another adhesion,' Marco murmured. 'How did we miss it?'

'Here—right down here, by the rectum. It's not a Ladd's band, it looks more like post-infection adhesions. Look, you can see scarring on the surface of the bowel. Poor little thing. She's obviously been in more pain than anyone had realised.'

She freed the adhesions carefully, and then the gut relaxed and slithered easily into a more natural and open position.

She felt her shoulders drop, and she saw Marco's sag with relief as well.

'Good,' she said. 'That's better.'

'Yes. It was a little resistant yesterday, but I thought we'd got it in the end. Obviously not all of it.'

'No, but it was really hard to see. I wish we'd done this yesterday so she didn't have to go through it twice, but I really thought we'd got it all. Still, it's done now,' she said, and stepped back, straightening her shoulders briefly.

He met her eyes. 'Are you OK?'

'Yes, I'm fine. Would you like to close?'

He smiled at her, his eyes creasing over his mask. 'If you like. Or you could close and I could put the sutures in Wuzzle.'

She smiled back at him and shook her head slowly.

'Have I ever told you what a softie you are?' she murmured, and she was rewarded with a low, sexy chuckle that sent tiny shivers up her spine. 'Go on, you close, and do Wuzzle,' she told him. 'I've got a ton of admin to do and I haven't had time for lunch yet.'

'Don't forget I'm feeding you tonight.'

'Only if Daisy's OK. Otherwise I'll stay.'

'She'll be fine. I'll come and find you when she's in Recovery.'

'Do that. I'll talk to Olive—and Dan, if he's around.'

Marco growled under his breath, and Alice just shrugged and left him to it. Dan would do what Dan would do, and it was Olive's problem, not theirs. All they could do was support the family as well as they could, and get Daisy better, and hopefully she was now on the road to recovery and a much, much brighter future.

CHAPTER FOUR

THEIR DINNER WAS postponed and Marco stayed in the hospital again overnight, but Daisy was doing well in PICU after her second operation and the next day they felt they could relax a little, so they rescheduled for seven.

Alice rang the bell right on the dot, and he opened the front door and she stepped inside and looked around curiously.

'Wow, what a fabulous house! I love all the period features.'

'Thank you. I like it. It was a bit of a run-down mess when I got it, but I've had a lot of work done over the last fourteen years, bits here and there, and now I can just enjoy it. Come on through to the kitchen.'

She followed him, taking the original encaustic floor tiles in the entrance hall with the intricate border pattern round the edges, the mahogany banister rail that curved gracefully upwards, the cherubs supporting the plaster arch spanning the hall—a much grander version of her own more simple arch—and then they walked through into the kitchen and time-travelled forward about a hundred and fifty years.

'Wow!' she said, craning her neck to look at the skylights where the room had been extended at the side, the double doors out of the end of the dining area, the acres of gleaming integrated appliances to the right set in a wall of cupboards, and jutting out as a divider between the two parts of the room was a pale granite worktop over base units painted a soft, muted grey.

How had he possibly afforded a house like this smack in the middle of Cambridge? Family money? Maybe. He'd said they did good weddings and everyone knew weddings didn't come cheap.

She ran her fingers over the granite and sighed. 'Oh, Marco, I love this room.'

He laughed softly. 'I love it, too, but it's a bit of a self-indulgence, rather like the rest of the house.'

'Well, why not, if you like it? It's not that big.'

'It's bigger than it looks. It has five bedrooms—well, no, not really. It has a loft conversion with an en suite and a fantastic view, which I use for guests, and I have one as a study and another as a dressing room, and then there's my room and another spare but, yes, it is ridiculous, before you say it.'

She bit her lip but the laughter bubbled out anyway. 'I wasn't going to be so rude, but I thought mine was outrageously expensive, and it's nothing like as big or as gorgeous as this.'

'It wasn't always gorgeous. I've had it a long time, and it was a bargain,' he said, taking things out of the fridge. 'And anyway, I've rented it out to bring in an income for a lot of the time and put the money back into doing it up. It's an investment.'

He'd turned towards the hob and placed a pan on it, and she stared at his back, slightly shocked by that last throwaway comment. 'It's your *home*, Marco.'

He shrugged. 'It can be both. And, yes, it's definitely my home. It's good to be back in Cambridge again, I'm enjoying it. I'm looking forward to the summer. The garden's beautiful, and it takes a lot of work but it's relaxing. It's my detox for the mind.'

'I thought that was running?' she said, settling herself on a high stool on the other side of the granite peninsula so she could watch him as he worked.

'That, too,' he said with a grin. 'Can I get you a drink?'

* * *

He put the food down in front of her with a twinge of concern. He'd found the recipe on the internet, ordered the ingredients and had them delivered to the hospital and spent the last half-hour throwing it together.

It was a sort of minced chicken and sautéd *cavolo nero* stir fry with an Italian twist, and just because he was starving he'd cooked some pasta for himself to serve with it, but he wondered if it might be too much for her delicate stomach.

'Wow, this is tasty,' she said, to his relief, and bit by bit, while they talked about this and that and not a lot, she ate it all. Then finally she pushed her plate away and smiled at him.

'OK?'

She gave a little laugh. 'More than OK, Marco. It was delicious. Thank you. I didn't realise how hungry I was. I've got so used to it, but it doesn't normally make me feel ill.'

'I guess that's because you're not normally pregnant,' he said drily as he gathered up the plates. 'Come and sit down, I'll put the kettle on and we can have tea. Peppermint would be my guess?'

She laughed again. 'I'm sorry, I'm a bit predictable. Do you know what I'd really like, though, while the kettle boils? A guided tour of your house.'

He frowned for a second, his mind running over the state he'd left the bedroom in, the bathroom—and then he shrugged. 'I can't guarantee it's tidy. I haven't been here for two days and my cleaning team haven't been.'

'You have a *team*?' she asked, her eyes widening.

'Not like that. A couple. They come once a week for an hour and run the vacuum cleaner over and dust and clean the bathroom and kitchen, change the sheets, that sort of thing. I don't make a lot of mess so they rotate the rooms.'

He could hear her mind working and frowned. 'What?'

She shrugged. 'It would never occur to me.'

'What, to have a clean and tidy house?'

'No, to pay someone to do it. My grandmother still cleans her own house and she's eighty-seven.'

He felt his eyes widen, then thought of his own grandmother, his mother's mother, much the same age, still fiercely independent. Maybe they weren't so different, but he was pretty sure his sisters didn't know one end of the vacuum cleaner from the other. One of the benefits, or not, of a privileged upbringing.

He took her upstairs—tidy, to his relief, as it hadn't been a foregone conclusion—and showed her first the guest suite in the attic, then the main floor, with his study that was a little chaotic but a practical room, the spare room, and then finally his room with a balcony and a wonderful view through French doors over the garden.

He turned off the light and switched on the outside lights on the balcony, and they lit up the first part of the garden so she could see it through the sparkle of the falling rain.

'Oh, that's gorgeous! How long is it?'

He shrugged. 'I don't know, I've never measured it. There are several "rooms" that you have to pass through to get to the end, and each one has its own identity. I'll show you at the weekend, if you like—assuming you're not busy and it isn't pouring with rain.'

He switched off the outside light and turned, and she was just there, inches from him in the shadowed room, lit only by the light spilling from the landing. And the bed, his ridiculously self-indulgent super-king-size bed, was just *there*.

For a moment he stood there, so tempted to reach out and touch her, to draw her into his arms, to kiss her slowly, tenderly, lingering over every sip and nibble, and she looked up and met his eyes in the dim light and he was lost.

He reached for her at the same moment she

reached for him, taking her in his arms and touching his lips to hers—just lightly, nothing too intense, nothing hasty like before, but slow, tender, lingering…

He felt the tension between them tighten, felt it in her body as if it was his own, felt the need, the yearning—and then she stepped back out of his arms and turned and headed for the door, and the moment was gone.

'I expect the kettle's boiled now,' she said, and he wasn't sure if he'd imagined it, or if her voice sounded just a little bit strained.

He made them both tea with fresh peppermint, fragrant and delicate, and she sipped it gratefully, her hands cradling the mug as she blew on it and tried not to think about that vast bed just above them in his bedroom.

If she hadn't pulled away they might well have been lying in it now, making love the way he'd told her she deserved on the night of the gala, when they'd finally given up fighting it in the consulting room and all but torn each other's clothes off in their haste. Well, she had, anyway.

His kiss tonight couldn't have been more different.

Why had he kissed her like that, so gently, so delicately, almost soothingly? Except it hadn't soothed her at all but, oddly, it had wound the tension inside her even tighter.

She'd told herself he was only being so caring because of the baby, but his kiss hadn't felt like that at all—instead, the tenderness of it had been so unexpected, so loving, almost as if he cherished her—her, not the baby—and that had confused her completely, when frankly she was confused enough.

'So, you've got a day-case list tomorrow morning,' she said to break the silence that seemed to be stretching to eternity.

'Yes, I have. I need to be in early to go over the notes.'

'Anything interesting?'

'Not really, I don't think. All pretty routine stuff. A couple of endoscopies, that sort of thing. Nothing exciting, which is good because I want to be on hand for Daisy.'

'Yes, I'm still worried about her. I'm much happier now than I was, but still. I might go back to the hospital and spend the night there, just in case.'

'There's no need. I can go in if necessary, but I don't think it will be, and I've left instructions for them to ring me if they're concerned. I've left my stuff in the on-call room I used for the last two nights just in case, so it might as well be me.'

She didn't argue. Frankly, although she'd eaten everything he'd given her and felt better for it, she knew the morning would be less than lovely.

She drained her cup and put it down on the coffee table.

'That was delicious. Thank you—not just for the supper, but for looking after me, and for taking the nights. I know I'm a bit ungracious when you nag me to eat and rest, but feeling like this doesn't come easily and I could never have cooked that for myself.'

'You're not ungracious, and you're very welcome.'

'You're a liar. I have been less than grateful.'

'Your independent streak a mile wide?'

She laughed softly and chose not to answer that one. 'I ought to go.'

His eyes met hers over the coffee table as they both stood up. 'You could always stay,' he said softly, his eyes curiously tender, and for a second she dithered, the memory of their kiss tempting her almost beyond reason, but then common sense cut in again and she shook her head. The last thing she needed was an audience first thing in the morning when she was at her worst.

'I don't think that's such a good idea. And anyway, you've got an early start tomorrow and mornings aren't good for me at the moment. I wouldn't want to put you off your breakfast.'

'That's not likely,' he said with an understanding smile. 'But whatever. It's your choice. Have you got your car here, or do you want me to drive you home?'

'No, but I can walk, it's not far.'

'But it's raining, and I don't like the idea of you walking around the city at night alone.'

She nearly laughed at that. 'Marco, I'm thirty-seven! I'm not stupid.'

'No, but you are a woman and that makes you vulnerable, and I'd never forgive myself if something happened to you, so if it's all the same with you, I will take you home.'

She smiled then and gave in, knowing she was never going to win the argument and not really wanting to, anyway, as it was raining. 'Thank you. I'd love a lift, I haven't got my mac. It was dry when I left home.'

He showed her out to the car, drove the short distance to her house and pulled up outside. It would have been so easy to reach out to him again, to lean over and kiss that firm, mobile mouth that showed every flicker of his feelings.

Not a good idea, because then she'd let herself fall in love with him and she didn't know him well enough yet. She had to trust him before she could dare to let that happen, and she wasn't quite there yet.

She reached for the door handle instead, and he got out of his side, came round to her and walked her to the door, then as she put her key in the lock and opened the door she turned back to thank him and his hand cupped her cheek.

'Goodnight, *tesoro*,' he murmured. 'Sleep well.'

His mouth brushed hers, the lightest, sweetest touch that sent fire searing through her body, and then before she could change her mind he got back into the car and raised his hand in farewell as he drove away.

She swallowed her disappointment and told herself it was probably just as well. They had to forge a friendship that would last throughout their baby's childhood and beyond, and a messy affair could compromise that. Ignoring the wails of regret from her body and her heart, she went inside, closed the door and went to bed alone.

It was strange, how simple and somehow cramped her house seemed to be after spending time in Marco's.

It felt—unfriendly? Surely not. She loved it, she'd chosen everything in it, and she liked it. But oddly, after last night at his, this morning it felt empty and soulless, and she realised she felt lonely.

She'd *never* felt lonely in her life! Well, only once or twice, if you didn't count the time after she'd revealed her diagnosis to the man who'd trashed her already fragile body confidence. She'd certainly felt lonely then, but somehow grateful for it, because she wasn't going to say or do anything to hurt herself, and being lonely wasn't a bad thing in comparison to the hurt he'd inflicted.

But Marco had never hurt her, never said anything cruel or unkind or other than gently teasing. Could she let herself fall in love with him? Did she dare?

Maybe…

And if she did, would they end up living in his beautiful home? She could almost picture it, picture their baby on the floor in the relaxed living space beyond the kitchen, lying on a mat and kicking her legs.

Her legs? Or his?

Her hand slid down and lay over her abdomen, still board-flat, of course, at this stage. Flatter even than usual, with her loss of appetite. Without Marco she'd be fading away, she realised, and she made herself eat breakfast although it was the last thing she wanted to do.

It worked, of course. She had scrambled

egg again, with avocado this time and a good scrunch of salt over the top, and by the time she reached the hospital she was feeling almost human. She was missing her exercise routine, but for now she didn't feel up to it and anyway, she was busy and worried about Daisy.

She found Marco at the little girl's bedside in PICU, carefully examining Wuzzle. He was listening to the teddy's heart with his stethoscope, and then Daisy's, and then he put the stethoscope on Daisy and let her listen to his own heart.

And she smiled, which made Alice's eyes well up.

'Morning, all,' she said brightly, and as he turned his head and looked at her, Daisy pulled a strange face.

'Your heart just went faster,' Daisy said innocently, her voice drowsy from medication.

Did it? That was interesting…

'That must be because Alice crept up on us and made me jump.'

Daisy giggled sleepily, and he retrieved his stethoscope and slung it round his neck, throwing Alice a wry grin.

'Have you come to check up on me?'

'No, I've come to see how Daisy is.'

'Daisy's doing well, aren't you, Daisy?' he asked her, and the little girl nodded.

'I'm a bit sore and a bit thirsty, but Marco says I can have little drinks now and I'll be better soon and my tummy won't hurt any more then.'

'We hope not,' Alice said with a smile. 'That's why we had to operate on you again, to make you better, even if it doesn't feel like it now. How's Wuzzle doing?'

'He's getting better, too. He slept all night.'

'Oh, that's really good. I am pleased.' Her eyes flicked back to Marco and for some reason her heart tumbled in her chest.

'So, shall we get on with the rest of the day?' she asked briskly. 'I thought you had day cases?'

'I do, but they're not here yet, it's only seven-thirty.'

Was it really? She hadn't even looked at her watch, not since she'd woken up and run to the bathroom, but thinking about it Evie wasn't at her post in ICU reception yet.

'Don't you need to read the notes?'

'Done it. I'm super-efficient, Alice. Firing on all cylinders.'

'So I can see,' she said drily, but she couldn't stop the smile. 'That must be why your heart's revving up.'

His mouth quirked and he kissed his fingertip and pressed it to the tip of Daisy's nose.

'Byebye, *piccolo*. I'll see you later, OK? And remember, only tiny sips of water.'

She nodded, and Marco joined Alice and they walked towards her office. 'Any sign of her parents this morning?' she asked, because it worried her that they hadn't been at Daisy's bedside.

'Yes, her mother was there, she went off to have breakfast, and her father's going to pop in later. I got the feeling she wasn't happy but he has no choice, she says. If he doesn't work, the company will fold and there are a lot of people relying on him. She seems very understanding but she's finding it tough, doing it all alone.'

'Of course she is. And I don't think Daisy's happy. I think she wants to see much more of her father.'

'I think they both do. So, how are you today?' he asked as he shut the door of her office behind them, and she laughed.

'Thoroughly average, thank you. I'm struggling to understand how people can have more than one child.'

'Because women definitely aren't the weaker sex,' he said drily. 'Men would never do it twice. On the subject of children, by the way, Ivy's been admitted for further tests. She's in a little family suite so Theo can keep an eye on her, and Madison Archer is due to arrive soon.'

'Ah, yes, the American diagnostician he managed to collar.'

'Yup. I think he's pinning a lot of hope on her, so let's hope she lives up to his expectations. From what he was saying last night, it's all pretty vague and he has no idea what on earth can be wrong with her.'

'Last night?'

He grinned ruefully. 'Yeah. I spent the night here in the end. I wanted to be close to Daisy, just in case—you know.'

'I do. I wish I'd known, I spent half the night worrying.'

'You don't need to worry.'

She rolled her eyes. 'Marco, that's like telling me I don't need to breathe. I can't help it.'

The grin widened into a wry smile. 'No, me, too. Anyway, so Theo and I chatted about Ivy for a while, and then we talked about the PAT dog I told you about, and I'm going to contact Alana and ask if she and Doodle can come in soon and visit Ivy. And I thought maybe Daisy would benefit, as well. She's going to be here for another couple of weeks, I would think.'

'Yes, she will. I'm not letting her go until she's entirely right and eating normally. Ditto Amil Khan. He might like to meet the dog, too. I take it Doodle is civilised?'

Marco laughed, his eyes crinkling. 'Civilised?

Yes, he's civilised. He's immensely gentle, and utterly lovely. He's like the softest teddy bear you've ever felt, and he's warm and cuddly and he has the biggest, daftest eyes in the world. He's just a sweetheart.'

'Have you talked to his owner yet?'

'No. I wanted to get the OK from Theo first, but I'll ring her this morning.'

'What, in between your day cases and all your other duties?'

'That's the one,' he said with a cheeky grin, and waggling his fingers at her he left her to deal with the mountain of admin that was waiting for her.

She didn't mind. It meant she could sit quietly in her office, sipping chilled water and nibbling on bland, salty snacks that she wouldn't normally touch but which seemed to be the only thing that kept her going, but she found herself unable to concentrate.

Daisy was clearly missing her father, didn't see nearly enough of him. Was this what was in store for their child, to feel cheated on a daily basis because his or her parents weren't together?

But apart from that one night, and Marco's constant nagging to her to eat or rest, there was nothing between them. No, that wasn't quite true. He'd kissed her yesterday in his bedroom, and asked her to stay, and she'd said no and he'd kissed her again when he'd taken her home. If she'd stayed, they would have made love, but would it have made a difference? Would it have brought them closer to a real, potentially lasting relationship, or stirred up the embers and set light to them again, just when it was all under control?

She had no idea, and there was a bit of her about a mile wide that was reluctant to put it to the test. Being torn apart once by someone she'd thought loved her was enough. She wasn't going to let it happen again, and it was much, much too soon to take anything for granted with Marco.

She had another sip of water, put him out of her mind and turned her attention to the day.

Three hours later, by which time she'd seen three new outpatients and tackled a heap of admin, she had a call from Marco.

'Come down to main reception. There's someone I want you to meet.'

She glanced at her watch. She was about to go for lunch anyway, so she could go that way. 'OK. Going to give me any clues?'

'Nope.'

She rolled her eyes, told him she'd be there in two minutes and made her way down to the glass-fronted circular reception area in the centre of the hospital. As she came out of the lift, she could see Marco standing with a young blonde woman on the far side of a group of sofas, and she made her way towards them, her curiosity piqued.

'Marco.'

He glanced across at her and smiled, and as she took the last few steps something pale gold and fluffy wafted across the floor by the sofa. Another step further and the waving fluff attached itself to the tail of an even fluffier body as the dog—at least she assumed it was a dog!—got to its feet and turned a hapless, tongue-lolling smile in her direction.

'Oh—you have to be Doodle!' she said with a laugh, and walking round the end of the sofa she stooped and fondled the softest head she'd ever felt. 'Oh, you soft, soft thing,' she crooned, staring down into melting brown doggy eyes that begged her to pour out her worries.

'Oh, he's so sweet,' she said, straightening up and meeting the smiling eyes of the blonde woman on the other end of the lead. 'Hi. You must be Alana. I'm Alice.'

She shook hands, her left hand still fondling Doodle's ears, and then she felt a weight settle against her left leg as Doodle sat down at her side, one surprisingly heavy foot resting on hers as if to anchor her there. She was more than happy to be anchored.

'Oh, Marco, you were absolutely right, he's gorgeous! Has Theo met him yet?'

Marco shook his head. 'No, not yet. He's just making a phone call and he's coming down—ah, here he is. If Doodle passes his test, he's going up to see Ivy.'

Alice smiled and gave Doodle one last fondle. 'I can't see how he could possibly fail. He's the most gorgeous thing I've ever met.'

Marco arched a brow and his mouth twitched. 'I could take offence at that,' he said lightly, and she chuckled.

'Seriously? The dog's way cuter. Right, I have to go for lunch. Lovely to meet you, Alana. I hope it goes well and you can join the team. I'm sure Daisy would adore Doodle—he's just like her teddy, Wuzzle, only even cuddlier, and the poor little thing could do with all the friends she can get.'

'Well, she'll certainly have a friend in Doodle,' Alana promised, and Alice left them just as Theo joined the group.

She headed towards the cafeteria, and a quick glance over her shoulder showed Theo crouching down, the dog sitting up with his paws on Theo's shoulders, nose to nose.

She had to smile. It looked like love at first

sight, and never mind Ivy, Theo could do with some love in his life right now and a therapy session with Doodle might be just the ticket for both of them.

'So how did it go with Doodle?'

Marco perched a hip on the corner of her desk and smiled a little sadly. 'Ivy adored him. Theo said it was the first time she'd really smiled in weeks, and he was pretty choked.'

She tutted softly. 'Oh, poor Ivy. So I take it Theo was convinced?'

'Yes, absolutely. He's going to ask if she can come every day for a short while and he's making a very generous donation to the Pets As Therapy charity, which, knowing Theo, doesn't surprise me, so I'm pretty sure we'll be seeing a lot more of her soon.'

'Won't Doodle get fed up with all that cuddling?' she asked, but Marco just laughed.

'I doubt it. He lives for cuddles and he just adores children.'

'How come Alana's got time?'

He shrugged. 'She's got a grooming business and she trains dogs, so a lot of her work is in the evenings, and she has staff to do the grooming so she can do the thing she loves, which is working with children. She's never said anything, but I get the impression children aren't on the cards for her. I think she might have had cancer as a teenager, which is how she got involved with this, so she's been doing it for years now—maybe ten? Doodle's her second dog. Her old dog's retired now from the cuddling, but she was a sweetie, too.'

Alice tipped her head on one side and tried to stifle a pang of what felt remarkably like jealousy. 'It sounds as if you know her quite well.'

He shook his head. 'No, not really. I met her when I was working locally a few years ago, and I bump into her every now and again out walking the dogs in the morning.'

'And she gave you her number?'

He peered closely at her and laughed. 'Are you jealous, Alice?'

She felt herself colour slightly. 'No, of course I'm not, don't be ridiculous. It just seemed—odd, that's all.'

'Not odd. I know her name, I know she has a grooming parlour, I know where it is, I looked it up and got her number. It's not rocket science, Alice. Or subterfuge. She's just an acquaintance.'

And now she felt stupid. 'Sorry. I wasn't quizzing you, it just seemed as if you knew her rather better than that,' she said, making it even worse, and giving up, she grabbed the open file on her desk, slapped it shut and stood up. 'Right,

I need to review some test results and do a ward round. Are you coming, or are you going to sit there all day and do nothing?'

He got lazily to his feet, tipped up her chin and laughed softly into her face as he stooped and dropped a kiss on her lips.

'God forbid I should pause for a minute. I only started work at five this morning,' he said drily, and opened the door for her in a display of courtesy that made her feel even more grumpy and ungracious.

Which just annoyed her even more.

CHAPTER FIVE

ALICE THOUGHT THE weekend would never come.

She'd been struggling with the early mornings and the relentless routine, made harder by the fact that, until it was blindingly obvious, she had no intention of telling anyone about the baby. It was hard to find time to eat, never mind rest, and because no one knew about the baby she found herself putting on an act, pasting on a cheerful face when she just wanted to crawl into a corner and sleep for a week.

And then, finally, it was the weekend. Daisy was improving, so was Amil, none of the other patients were a worry, so when Saturday morning dawned she took it easy, giving herself the luxury of surfacing slowly and gently. She ate a small but nutritious breakfast, surprised herself by keeping it down and decided to go for a walk.

Not a run. She didn't feel up to that, and she certainly didn't want to work out in the gym at the hospital, but she needed to do something, and getting out in the late October sunshine was exactly what she needed.

It was a glorious day, and she strolled down to the river and along the Backs behind King's College Chapel and the colleges that bracketed it. She hardly ever took time to do this, to study the stunningly beautiful architecture of the old university buildings, or to walk beside the river and watch the ducks swimming along without a care in the world. She found a café not far away and had a peppermint tea out in the sunshine on the deck overlooking the river in the company of the dog walkers, the only ones rash enough to brave the great outdoors this late in the year.

Then she turned and walked back towards her house, her feet straying off course and leading her past Marco's house. She hesitated opposite it, wondering if it would be rude to knock on the door, but then she heard the rhythmic thud of feet on the path behind her. She stepped to one side, but the feet slowed and came to a halt.

'*Buon giorno.*'

She turned and found a heaving, muscular chest just inches from her face, the damp T-shirt clinging lovingly to it as it rose and fell with every breath. The chest she'd raked her nails down—

'Good morning,' she said, hauling her eyes up to his. 'Had a good run?'

'Long one. I've been out into the country—about twenty-five K or so? I don't know. Longer than usual, but it was such a beautiful day I just kept going.' He cocked his head on one side. 'Fancy a coffee?'

She recoiled slightly at that, and he must have seen because he grimaced in a smiley way.

'Sorry. Peppermint tea, then?'

'Don't you need to shower?'

He laughed and took a step back. 'Was that a hint? I can shower quickly, *bella.* Give me five minutes. Come on, because it's such a lovely day, and I want to show you my garden.'

He didn't wait for an answer, just jogged across the road, unlocked his front door and stood holding it while he waited for her. She shrugged, shook her head laughingly in despair and followed him in.

He showered quickly, as he'd promised, although he would happily have stood there for several more minutes being pounded by the deluge of hot water streaming over his aching muscles. Still, at least he'd washed the sweat off.

He towelled himself roughly dry, pulled on clean jeans and a sweater and went down to the kitchen. Alice was perched on a stool at the breakfast bar, flicking through a recipe book. Looking at the pictures, he imagined, since it was Italian and he knew she didn't speak a word of his mother tongue.

'Seen anything interesting?' he asked, and she glanced up, a fleeting expression on her face that vanished before he could analyse it.

'Not really.' She shut the book and swivelled round to look out of the wall of glass at the end of the room. 'Your garden looks lovely.'

'It is. Peppermint tea?'

'Please.'

She'd boiled the kettle already, he realised, and nipped some shoots off the pot of mint on the windowsill. He rinsed them under the tap, put them into mugs and poured the boiling water over them. The fresh, clean scent rose in the steam, and he slid a mug across the work-top towards Alice.

'Here you go. So—have you had any more thoughts about my sister's wedding?' he asked, propping himself up against the granite and blowing the steam off his mug.

She turned her head to look at him, then picked up her mug and swivelled back towards the garden again.

'Not really. Tell me more about it. How dressy is it? How formal? How many people?'

He laughed gruffly and put the mug down. 'I have no idea. Two hundred?'

'Two hundred?' she said, glancing back at him, her eyes widening.

He shrugged. 'Maybe more. At least half of them will be family in one way or another, then some business contacts, neighbours, family friends, and their own friends. There'll be a lot of people there.'

'So where would we stay?'

'At my family house or somewhere on the estate. Where else?'

'I have no idea, that's why I'm asking.' She swivelled back to face him, her eyes a little wary. 'Will they be expecting us to share a room?'

He shook his head. 'No, not if I tell them we aren't together, and I don't want to invite any unnecessary speculation about our relationship at this point—and I certainly don't think they need to know about the baby yet.'

'No. No, absolutely not. So—um—the dress code?'

He shrugged. 'The usual—I'll be wearing a suit, of course, probably a tux. You could wear the dress you wore for the gala, so long as you cover it with a jacket or a wrap or something for the ceremony. And you'll need something for the night before. We'll have a dinner just for family, but it'll be quite dressy. Then the next day there'll be a civil ceremony in the town hall in the morning, followed by a religious ceremony in the church on the estate and then an endless round of eating and drinking and dancing until everyone gives up and goes to bed in the small hours. Then the following day it'll all start again, with a huge lunch for everyone before they set off home.'

She looked thoughtful, and not in a good way.

'That sounds pretty full-on,' she said, and he laughed.

'It's an Italian wedding. They are full-on. The wedding itself is on Sunday, the family dinner on Saturday, and we'd fly back on Monday afternoon.'

'Monday? But what about work?'

'We're booked off until Tuesday.'

'We? I haven't said yes yet!'

'You didn't need to. We have no new patients booked in, there's a short day-case list on the Tuesday and otherwise nothing apart from the usual routine, and we'll get back on Monday afternoon in time for a quick ward round and a catch-up. We won't need more than usual weekend cover, and we'll be back in on Tuesday to do any discharges. You've got an outpatients' list, and I've got the day cases.'

'You've got it all worked out, haven't you?'

'Yes, of course. For me, at least, because I was always going.'

She looked away again, turning her attention back to the peppermint tea so he couldn't read her eyes.

'So—if I come, do I really need to be there for the night before?' she asked after a slight pause.

'Yes,' he said firmly. 'It's remote, and we'll travel together. It's easier that way than trying to get there under your own steam. If you prefer, you could miss the dinner and eat in your room, but it's pretty pointless. Nobody bites.'

'Marco, I don't speak a word of Italian.'

He shrugged. 'That's fine. They all speak English, some better than others but enough to get by. You won't be isolated. And anyway, I'll be there. I won't throw you to the wolves, Alice.'

Wolves? Wrong choice of word, probably because it didn't seem to reassure her at all, so he put his mug down again, let the subject drop and headed for the doors at the end. 'Come and see the garden,' he suggested, and she slid off the stool, put her mug down beside his and followed him out.

He was right, it was a beautiful garden.

The first part close to the house was designed for overflow from the house and to bring the outside in, and although they weren't in flower she could see small hedges of lavender edging the paving, and behind them, some still in bloom, were roses.

She reached over to smell one and her foot brushed the lavender below and released a soft wave of scent from the foliage. It must be heavenly in the summer, she thought, and wondered if she'd be there to see it.

Not if she kept holding him at arm's length, but he'd just been so emphatic about telling his family they weren't together in order to avoid unnecessary speculation, and he clearly didn't want to mention anything about the baby.

She followed him up the garden, her hand sliding down protectively over her abdomen, her fingers splayed low over where the baby—their baby—was lying.

Was it really only six weeks tonight since the gala? How her life had changed. Not on the outside. The baby was tiny still; at this stage it was barely recognisable as a human foetus, hardly the size of a kidney bean—but not too small to make its presence felt in multiple tiny changes to her body. Yet nobody looking at her would know the fundamental nature of what was brewing, the earthquake that would shake up her life and change everything, with the baby at its epicentre.

It would change Marco's life, too, of course, which was one reason he wanted her to go to the wedding, to meet his family, the baby's grand-parents and uncles and aunts and cousins. Hundreds of them, by the sound of it.

Was she going to go?

Maybe. There was a massive part of her that was curious about his family, about the place he'd grown up, the people he'd shared his early life with. She'd get to meet the people who were related to her baby. That was a plus point.

The other plus point, of course, was that she'd get to spend time with him away from the hospital, time out from reality when she could maybe see if they might have a future. Because they would have a future together, tied together for ever by their child, whether they were living as a couple or not. He'd be a part of her life for the next twenty years, at least, and she wasn't sure how that felt.

Exciting? Challenging? Terrifying?

She was so used to living alone, so used to making her own decisions, dictating her own timetable, choosing her hobbies, her food, her colour schemes, what she watched on the TV—all that would change if she was in a relationship. Did she want it to change?

Or did she want to be like Olive Lawrence, struggling to bring up a child with a largely absent and remote father figure lurking in the background?

Not that she could imagine Marco lurking.

No. He'd be at the centre of his child's life, playing a full and active role, and constantly underfoot—

'So, what do you think of it?'

She realised they'd reached the end of the garden, and she hadn't heard a word he'd said to her. She looked up and met his eyes, and he sighed softly and cupped her face in his hands and feathered the lightest kiss across her lips, a soft frown puckering his brow.

'Don't look so troubled, Alice. Is it the wedding?'

She shrugged. 'I don't know. The wedding, the baby—all of it. I'm afraid I'll lose it, worried about what the future will bring—it's all the unknowns, really.'

He tsked gently, and folded her into his arms, cradling her head against his broad, solid chest. She could hear his heart beating under her ear, thought of Daisy listening to it and laughing when it speeded up.

Had that really been because of her?

'Come to the wedding with me,' he urged softly. 'It will give us some time away from all of this, time just to be together, get to know each other away from work. Neutral territory.'

She eased out of his arms with a little laugh.

'Hardly that. It's your family home! I'll be like a fish out of water.'

'Nonsense. It'll be fine, *carissima*, believe me. Besides,' he went on, his eyes twinkling with mischief, 'I need you there to protect me from all the single women who'll be gathering round me like a school of piranhas.'

That made her laugh again, properly this time. 'You really do have a massive ego,' she teased, but he shook his head, the laughter fading from his eyes.

'No. They're after my status, my family's money. They don't care about me, they don't know me. It's all about what they can get for themselves.'

She frowned. 'That's horrible.'

'It is. But it's the reality.'

'Does your family really have that much money and status?' she asked, slightly shocked, and he gave a wry laugh and turned back towards the house. His ridiculously extravagant and beautiful house.

'Yes. Sadly. It doesn't interest me, not in the slightest, but it's there, and it's one of the reasons I needed to get away and just be myself, be a doctor, heal kids, because that's who I am.'

'And they didn't understand?'

'No. They didn't. Well, except my grandmother, my mother's mother. Nonna understands—not that she approves of the way I did it, but at least she can see why and she's hugely proud of me now. She's the only one who is. I think you'll like her.'

'She'll be there?'

'Yes, of course. Her granddaughter's wedding? She wouldn't miss it for the world. And I have to say she and my baby sister Annalisa, the bride, are the only two reasons I'm going, because I can't bear to hurt either of them.'

He opened the door for her, and they went back into the kitchen.

'Come, I'll show you where I grew up,' he said, and led her up the stairs to his study. He pulled up a chair, turned on the laptop and with a few keystrokes went onto a website.

'This is where I lived,' he said, and clicked through the gallery of photos—a beautiful, classic Tuscan stone house set high on a hill with stunning views all around it.

She felt her jaw sagging. 'It's huge!'

'It's a *castello*—an ancient castle. Parts of it are probably over twelve hundred years old, but nobody's sure and it's been extended so many times, a bit on here, another bit on there. It's been in the family for over five hundred years, and everyone's put their mark on it. It's surrounded by a sprinkling of small villas and farmhouses, which have been turned into guest accommodation to supplement the estate. We grow grapes to make our own wine, olives for oil, there are chestnut woods that are harvested, sheep that are milked for cheese-making, and we do tourism. Tours of the cantina—the winery—and tours of the estate and surrounding area. It's a big family business.'

'And they wanted you to be part of it?'

'They wanted me to run it.'

'But you're a doctor!'

'I know, but I'm also the firstborn son. It's my *duty* to stay and carry on the family tradition. That's more important.'

She sat back and stared at him. 'Seriously? They thought that was more important than following your heart?'

'Yes. All except Nonna.' He closed the computer and turned to face her, his eyes a little bleak. 'So you understand why I had to leave.'

'Of course I understand! Oh, Marco—don't they realise what you'd have been giving up? How many children would have suffered if you'd given in to them?'

He shrugged. 'There are other doctors who could have done my job. They have no other firstborn son.'

'But it's not like it's the monarchy! Don't they have any other sons or daughters who want to carry the torch?'

He laughed. 'Yes, of course. Two of my brothers and one of my sisters are heavily involved. That's not the point. It was *my* job, *me* who was meant to do it. Not my brother Gio, who's a Master of Wine and a first-class sommelier. He has a nose for wine like nobody I've ever met, but he's not good enough for them, and neither is Raffaello, who has a first-class business brain and has done a huge amount for the family business. It should have been me, despite the fact that I don't really like wine and couldn't give a damn about business or earning money.'

'That sounds—I don't know. Medieval! It's awful!'

He shook his head, his laughter weary this time. 'No, it's not awful, they're just so steeped in tradition that they don't know how to escape from it. It's worked for generations, and then I come along and spoil it.'

He leant forward and took her hands. 'Please come with me. I love it there, and I love them, but they suffocate me. Come with me and let me show you what is so much a part of me that even I can't deny it completely. And meet my *nonna.* She'll love you, Alice. She's a proud, strong woman, so much like you, but she's getting old now and she won't last for ever. I really want her to meet the mother of my child.'

Because she might not live long enough to

see the baby? It was a plea from the heart and she couldn't refuse him that.

She nodded. 'OK. I'll come with you and meet your grandmother and see where you grew up. You obviously love it, and it might help me to understand more about the father of my child if I know what moulded you.'

For a moment he didn't reply, then he bowed his head slightly in acknowledgement. 'Thank you,' he murmured. His hands, still holding hers, squeezed gently, and he leant forward and touched his lips to hers.

It was a fleeting kiss, or meant to be, but she ended up in his arms and only a massive effort of will made her able to ease away before it escalated into something more.

'I need to go, Marco,' she said, but she couldn't hold his searching eyes, and after a moment he sighed and stood up, freeing her from her trance.

'Me, too. I want to go back to the hospital and check on Amil and Daisy, and one of my patients I should have discharged before the weekend who I wasn't happy enough to let go. But—maybe later? Can I cook you dinner?'

She was so tempted—ludicrously tempted—but she shook her head. 'I've got food in the fridge that needs eating,' she said, which was a lame excuse but the best she could come up with at such short notice, and it seemed to satisfy him. Maybe he was just being kind, following through on his promise to be there for her and help her through her pregnancy?

They went back downstairs, and he reached for the door and opened it.

'Take care, Alice. I'll see you tomorrow, maybe.'

'Maybe. I've got a lot of things to do.'

He nodded, his eyes somehow withdrawing, and his smile, when it came, didn't quite reach them.

'I'll see you on Monday, then,' he said, and she nodded and stepped out into the sunshine, but it had lost its magic, the light fading with the light in his eyes, and she felt a weight in her chest that was probably common sense but felt oddly like disappointment.

His phone rang at six the next morning, and he reached for it, blinking his eyes open as he scanned the screen.

Alice? At this time of the morning?

'Alice? Are you OK?'

'No.' Her voice had a slight shake in it, and he threw off the bedclothes and reached for his clothes. 'I—I've had a bleed. Nothing much, just a few spots, but—'

She broke off, and he rammed a hand through

his hair and sucked in a deep breath. 'OK. Where are you?'

'Where? Um—I'm at home.'

'Stay there. Unlock the front door and go and lie down on the sofa. I'm on my way.'

He cut off the call, threw on his clothes and was there in five minutes, grateful that the streets were deserted. Her door was unlocked and he pushed it open and called her name.

'In here,' she said, and he went into the sitting room and found her curled up at one end of the sofa, a blanket over her and her face streaked with tears.

'Oh, Alice...'

He gathered her up into his arms, his heart aching as she sobbed into his chest. Not for long. She only gave herself that luxury for a moment before she pushed him away and sniffed, her hands scrubbing the tears from her cheeks.

'So—what happened?'

'Nothing dramatic. I woke up, went to the loo and there were these spots of blood.'

'Anything since?'

She shook her head. 'I don't think so. I can't feel anything.'

'No pain anywhere?'

Again she shook her head. 'No. No pain, nothing. And I think I must still be pregnant because I still feel horribly sick, but I'm afraid to eat in case I need to go to Theatre.'

He frowned. 'It's a long time since I did any obstetrics, but I would think that's unlikely today. Maybe if you go on to miscarry they might need to do a D&C, but not just for a slight bleed. It would have to be a lot worse, I think. Mind if I have a feel of your abdomen, just to check it's not an ectopic or anything like that?'

She shook her head and rolled to her back, and he pressed very lightly, very carefully over her slender abdomen, pushing gently to see if it caused any pain, but she said there was none, to his relief.

'I think that rules out an ectopic,' he said, 'but I do think you need to go in.'

She nodded. 'Yes, that makes sense. So maybe I should try and eat something first.'

'What can I get you?'

She shrugged. 'I don't know. Cold water? There's some in the fridge. And maybe some fruit. There are some slices of mango in there, too.'

'OK.' He left her and went into the kitchen, put the kettle on, took the mango and water back to her and sat down by her feet. 'Have you done another pregnancy test?'

She shook her head. 'No. I've got one—I bought a double pack last week because it was all they had in the supermarket I went to, so there's one left over, but I didn't think about doing a test when I was in the bathroom. I just wanted to talk to you—'

Her voice cracked and he reached out and rested a hand gently on her hip. 'Don't be scared, Alice. I'm here. I'm not going anywhere. Well, maybe in the kitchen to have a coffee,' he said with a wry smile, and she smiled back.

'Thank you.'

'What for?'

'All sorts of things, but most specifically never drinking coffee in front of me. I know you miss it, and I do appreciate it.'

He laughed softly and got to his feet. 'It's not much of a sacrifice, *cara.*'

He went back to the kitchen, spooned ground coffee into a cafetière and took it, a mug and the kettle out into her garden to make it, closing the door behind him to stop the smell filtering in.

And while he waited for it to brew, he checked on the local NHS trust website for advice on threatened miscarriage in the first trimester.

Bingo. There was an early pregnancy assessment unit in Cambridge, which opened at eight-thirty on Sundays. Good.

He poured and drank his coffee, rinsed his mouth so he didn't breathe coffee fumes all over her and went back and told her about the clinic.

'I think you should go and see someone there,' he said, and she nodded.

'Will you come with me?' she asked, as if she'd seriously doubted that he would, and he frowned in disbelief.

'Alice, of course I'll come with you. This is my baby, too, and I'm as concerned as you are. Of course I'll come. I wouldn't dream of letting you go alone.'

Her shoulders drooped, as if she'd been afraid he'd leave her to it, and he knelt down beside her and put his arms around her, letting his head rest against hers.

'Don't be afraid, Alice,' he murmured. 'Lots of women have bleeding in the first trimester and go on to have a normal pregnancy.'

'And lots don't.'

'Shh. Let's cross that bridge when we get to it, hmm? If we do. And in the meantime, you need to eat.'

'I can't. I tried. The mango's too flavoured.'

'So what do you fancy?'

'Scrambled egg and avocado.'

He felt his eyebrow twitch and schooled his expression. 'With lots of salt, I imagine?'

Her smile was weak. 'How did you guess?'

It was delicious.

Well, delicious for something that hardly

tasted of anything except salt, but that was fine by her. She sat up and ate it, sipped the cup of hot water he'd brought her and then went upstairs to wash and dress and pack a bag to take to the hospital, just in case. She was conscious all the time of his presence in the house, the sound of his movements, his voice on the phone, the sound of water running in the kitchen as he rinsed the plates, the clatter of the dishwasher being loaded.

She smiled to herself, wondering how he managed to be so domesticated and yet still needed a cleaning team to keep his house in order. Although she could do with a visit from them. She'd hardly done anything this last week because she'd felt so tired, and the house was beginning to look a little unkempt.

She zipped on her boots, straightened up and her hand slid down, coming to rest over her baby.

'Please be all right,' she whispered, her heart suddenly flip-flopping at the thought that it might all go wrong. Might have *gone* wrong, and then she'd have lost not only the baby, but Marco, and all her dreams for the future...

She heard his tread on the stairs, a gentle tap on her bedroom door.

'Alice?'

She opened it and stepped straight into his

arms, resting her head against his heart. It was beating strongly, the rhythm steady, solid, comforting.

Would her baby have a heartbeat?

Please, let my baby be all right...

'Come on, *tesoro*,' he murmured. 'Don't worry. We'll do this together. I won't leave you, I promise.'

She straightened up, and he slid his hand down her arm and threaded his fingers through hers, and she felt his strength seeping into her, giving her the courage to do this, to go to the hospital and find out if they still had a baby.

What happened after that she couldn't worry about now, but for now she had him, and that was enough.

CHAPTER SIX

THEY WERE AT the hospital before the clinic opened, but they were second in the queue and she was called in almost immediately.

'Want me to come?'

She felt a flicker of alarm. 'Please.'

He took her hand, as if he could read that she needed the comfort of his touch, and all through her examination he was either beside her or she could feel his presence.

She was asked a whole raft of questions, most of which Marco had already asked her, including whether or not she'd had a positive pregnancy test and when her last period had been, and then the nurse took her blood pressure.

'It's a little high. Is that normal for you?'

'I have PCOS,' Alice told her. 'It's not normally high, though. I keep it controlled with diet and exercise, but that's gone out of the window a bit in the last week with the pregnancy sickness.'

'OK. It could just be worry, then, but that's what you're here for so let's try and give you some answers. Do you mind if I examine you?'

'No, of course not,' she said, lying down on the couch and wishing Marco was there to hold her hand, not seated on the other side of the curtain out of reach.

The examination was gentle but thorough and brought an element of good news, which was a relief.

'Well, your cervix is tightly closed, you don't appear to have any significant bleeding at the moment and there's no abdominal tenderness, so that's all good, but I do want you to have an ultrasound scan to see if we can find out a bit more about what's going on,' the nurse said, stripping off her gloves and helping her off the couch. 'Once you've had that done, depending on what they find you'll have blood tests and we'll arrange a follow-up or admit you, but let's start with the scan and see what that comes up with. You'll need a transvaginal scan, so you'll have to make sure you have an empty bladder, and while you're doing that, if you could get me a urine sample I'll do a quick pregnancy test on it while you wait.'

Alice nodded, tugged her clothes straight and went back to Marco, who was sitting quietly, his eyes watchful.

'OK?' he asked softly, and she nodded.

She was shown to a toilet, armed with a little pot for her urine sample, and when she came back she was sent back out to the waiting room. A couple of minutes later the nurse emerged with the news that the test was positive, which showed she still had pregnancy hormones in her body, and although she knew that didn't necessarily mean the baby was still alive, it gave her some hope.

Until she saw that tiny heart beating with her own eyes she wouldn't dare believe it, though, and it was an agonising ten more minutes before she was called through for her scan.

'Do you want me with you?' Marco asked as she stood up, and she nodded.

'Yes—definitely. Unless…'

'No. I want to be there.'

'Then come—please?'

She undressed and lay down under a blanket, and he sat beside her and took her hand, his eyes fixed on hers as the sonographer inserted the probe. An image popped up on the screen and she turned her head to see it, hanging onto him for dear life. Her grip on his fingers must have been painful, but she couldn't let go, couldn't relax so much as a hair until—

The image settled, and as a fast, rhythmic

whoosh, whoosh, whoosh filled the room, she felt his grip tighten.

'Is that—?' Marco asked, and she held her breath.

'That's your baby's heartbeat,' the sonographer told them with a smile, and the blurry little image blurred even more. 'It sounds good and strong. Look, this is the baby's head, and here's its heart—can you see it beating?'

Alice blinked hard to clear her vision, and there it was, a tiny bean of a thing, fatter at the head end, with a dark, pulsating blob in the centre, beating in time to the whooshing sound that filled the room.

'Oh...'

Was that her, or him? Both, she thought, staring at the screen, her heart swelling with love as she watched that bravely beating heart inside their tiny baby.

Marco removed his hand and fiddled with his phone for a second, and she realised he was recording it, filming the grainy little image, recording the sound of their baby's heartbeat as it filled the room with hope.

The sonographer took a few measurements, and smiled again. 'So, that's all looking good, spot on for eight weeks—did you say eight weeks today since your last period?'

'Something like that. Six weeks yesterday

is the only possible time it was conceived,' she said, feeling a little numb as she realised how much had happened deep inside her body in those six short weeks. Lying there watching her baby's heart pumping was like an out of body experience, and she felt strangely light-headed, as if she was floating…

'These little things here are the arm buds, one each side, so, and down here we have the leg buds—oh, and it's doing a little wiggle for you! How about that. Do you want a photo?'

'Yes,' they said in unison, and then a little while later, after a few more measurements had been taken, the sonographer said, 'Right, you're all done,' and the image vanished from the screen.

'Wow,' Marco said softly, breaking the breathless silence, and for the second time she adjusted her clothes and sat up, her body shaking all over as she slid off the couch to her feet.

'I'm still pregnant,' she said unsteadily, looking up into his eyes, and to her horror and embarrassment, she burst into tears.

'Oh, Alice,' he murmured, and then his arms wrapped her tight against his chest, his lips pressed to her temple, and she could feel the thudding of his heart through his chest wall. 'It's OK, *amore mio*, it's all right. Our baby's OK.'

She could hear his voice cracking, and she

tilted her head back and stared up into his eyes. His lashes were clumped together with tears, and as he bent his head and kissed her, she felt one fall on her cheek and mingle with her own…

'Better now?'

'Much better.'

Because she'd said she felt light-headed he'd got her a fruit tea and a banana in the café at the hospital, and they were still sitting there, armed with a follow-up appointment and the knowledge that their baby was still alive and seemed to be doing well, to her relief and his, too, she was sure of that now. She gave him a rueful smile. 'Thank you so much for coming with me.'

That seemed to shock him. 'Did you really imagine I'd let you do it alone, Alice? This is *my* baby, too. Of course I'm here.'

Her eyes welled again, and she nodded once more and looked down at her hands, twisting in her lap. 'I thought…'

'I know.' He reached out and took her hands, wrapping them in his and resting his head against hers. 'Come on, let's get out of here and take you home.'

He drove to his house, and as he cut the engine she turned and looked at him in surprise.

'This is your house.'

'Yes. I thought it would be better. I'll take you home if you'd rather, but I don't really want to leave you alone. I thought you could lie on the sofa and watch the birds in the garden while I work, and I can cook you lunch, if you like? I've got stuff in the fridge.'

She searched his eyes, not sure what she was looking for, but there was tenderness there in those rich brown depths and she nodded.

'That sounds nice. Thanks.'

'Don't keep thanking me, Alice. It's fine.'

It was fine, she realised as she followed him in. She didn't want to be alone, and she didn't want to be in her own house, she realised. It was nice enough, but Marco's house was more than that, it felt like a home, and hers had never felt as homely as his. Maybe because she'd moved in and started work and hadn't really had time to claim it, but Marco's taste and personality were stamped all over this house, and she loved it.

He settled her on the sofa, pampering her with plumped-up cushions and the softest, snuggliest throw tucked around her.

Not that it was cold in his house, but she felt chilled inside. Shock? Maybe, but that was slowly receding, leaving a sense of wonder.

'Can I see the recording?' she asked when he came back in with a glass of mint tea for her, and he sat down beside her, perching on the edge of the sofa, and turned it on so they could both watch it again.

Her finger reached out and hovered over the screen. 'It's so tiny.'

'It's a long time to the beginning of June.'

'It is. Just think, Daisy Lawrence was only three weeks older than this when her gut coiled the wrong way, but looking at it, how tiny and unformed it all is, it seems incredible that things don't go wrong more frequently. How can something so complex as a human being be so perfect so very often?'

'I have no idea. Life is a miracle, Alice. It never ceases to amaze me. Just listen to that.'

He played it again, the sound of their baby's heart filling the room, and she felt her eyes well with tears again.

'I never thought I'd ever hear that, my baby's heart beating. I could listen to it all day,' she said softly, and he handed her the phone and stood up, bending to drop a gentle kiss on her cheek.

'Be my guest. I'll go and see what I can find for lunch.'

She watched it over and over again, until the sound of their baby's heart became a part of her, a sub-rhythm playing quietly in the background as she fell asleep.

* * *

She was sleeping.

Good. She'd looked exhausted, racked with worry, and it wasn't over yet. Things could still go wrong, and he hadn't really registered until she'd told him she was bleeding just how much he cared, how very much the baby and Alice meant to him.

Far more than he'd imagined. Far more than was sensible, given her reluctance to let him into her life.

He retrieved his phone from the floor and left her to sleep, going back to the kitchen and turning down the oven. Lunch would keep, and a little longer in the oven wouldn't hurt it. He had plenty to do.

With one last look back at her, he went upstairs into his study, turned on his computer and settled down to work.

Her phone woke her, the sound penetrating her sleep and dragging her out of a strange and surreal dream in which she and Marco were walking along pushing a pram.

She groped in her bag, came up with the phone and glanced at the screen. Her mother.

She struggled into a sitting position and tapped the screen. 'Hi, Mum. How are you?'

'I'm fine, we're all fine. I just wondered how

you are. I haven't heard anything from you for ages and I thought it was time to touch base, that's all.'

'Oh. Yes, I'm sorry, I've been ridiculously busy.' She shifted herself more upright, propping herself up against the back of the sofa and staring out at the garden. The sun was shining, and she could see the last of the roses blooming bravely behind the little lavender hedge. They'd be in flower again when the baby was born, she thought, and then realised she needed to tell her mother—or at least some of it.

'Mum, there's something I need to tell you,' she said abruptly, cutting off her mother's ramblings about what her father had been up to in the garden. 'I'm having a baby.'

The gasp was followed by silence, and then a tiny sob. 'Oh, Alice! David! David, come here! Alice is pregnant! So, come on, tell us all about it. Who's the father? Is it that gorgeous Italian guy you're working with?'

How on earth had her mother worked that out? Alice knew she'd been all over the hospital website looking at the profiles of the staff, and she'd been fixated on Marco since day one. Rather like she had herself.

'Yes, it is, but don't get over-excited, Mum, I've got a long way to go,' she said, suddenly regretting telling her because she was going to misunderstand and jump to the conclusion it was all sunshine and roses and it might not be—there might not even be a baby if it all went wrong, which it still might.

What was she thinking? She shouldn't have told her yet, especially when Marco was still— no, not distant, he'd never been distant, and if he was, she only had herself to blame, because she'd been holding him at arm's length, she re- alised, but he'd been amazing today. It was just the cosy, sentimental dream she'd been woken from which had made her blurt it out, and now her mother was in a tizzy of excitement and it was way too soon for that.

'Mum, stop it! Listen. There isn't going to be a wedding or anything like that. We're not— together,' she said, for want of a better way to put it. 'Marco and I are just colleagues, friends, maybe, and he's going to be part of the baby's life but it was an accident, really, I never in- tended this to happen, but it has, and I thought you should know. I had a scan today, and—oh, his phone's gone. I was going to play you the recording of its heartbeat—'

'Here,' Marco said, appearing beside her and handing her the phone. He pressed the button to start it playing, and walked out into the kitchen, closing the door behind him.

She stared at the door, because there was

something about the way he'd closed it. Not hard, not loud, just—significant.

'Oh, darling, that's amazing,' her mother was saying tearfully as the recording came to an end, and Alice dragged her eyes off the door and answered a few more questions—how many weeks was she, when was it due, how was she feeling, was there anything she needed?

Only Marco, and from the way he'd shut that door it didn't look like that was happening any time soon. She answered the questions, said goodbye, hung up and got carefully to her feet.

Not together?

Dio, how could she say that after today? They'd waited together for news, held hands, gasped, cried—how was that *not together*?

He'd come down when he'd heard her voice, thinking he'd dish up their lunch as she was awake, but he'd never expected to hear that. Who was she talking to? Her mother, he thought. He might have heard her say that as he'd got to the bottom of the stairs. Right before she'd said they weren't *together*, just colleagues or maybe friends.

Colleagues? Friends? Maybe?

He felt gutted. Angry and frustrated and hurt and—just plain gutted that he meant so little to her, after all they'd been through this past week.

He'd thought they'd made some progress when she'd agreed to go with him to the wedding, but apparently not.

Damn. He wished he hadn't asked her now, wished he hadn't booked their flights last night, but that was ridiculous, because a thousand things could happen in the fortnight before the wedding, including, although he hoped not with all his heart, her losing the baby. The baby that, after the initial shock, had suddenly made him realise just how much he wanted to be a father. How much he wanted a family—but it seemed he might be alone in that.

'Oh, Alice, what do you want from me?' he sighed, propping his hands on the edge of the worktop and dropping his head forward, staring at the floor as if it held any answers.

It didn't.

His own head did, but none that he wanted to hear. He'd been going to ask her to move in with him, to live here with him in this house so he could look after her and they could start to build a life together—and not just because of the baby. Because he wanted her, needed her.

Loved her?

No, it was too soon for that, but he had his answer now, anyway, and without the humiliation of having to ask her and have it thrown back in his face, because it seemed that whatever Alice wanted from him, it wasn't togetherness.

He heard the door open and he straightened up as she came in.

'Your phone,' she said, handing it to him with a searching glance. 'Thanks for that. I was telling my parents about it. They're ridiculously over-excited.'

'Was that really wise, until you're sure your pregnancy's secure?' he said, probably not as tactfully as he could have put it but the truth, for all that, and she sucked in a breath and stepped back.

'I just—I wanted to tell them. It seemed like the right thing to do. You think I shouldn't have told them? Do you still think I'm going to lose it?'

The look on her face ripped a hole in his heart, and if he could have swallowed the words, he would have done. 'I have no idea, Alice,' he said heavily. 'I sincerely hope not. As for telling them, they're your parents, not mine, only you can be the judge of that. Look, I need to go to the hospital. There's a chicken casserole in the oven keeping hot. Help yourself. I won't be long.'

'Is everything OK?'

'Yes, it's fine, I just want to check on Daisy

and Amil and look over some paperwork before tomorrow's list. Help yourself to anything you need, and ring me if anything changes. I'll see you later.'

He almost kissed her goodbye, but thought better of it, pulling back into himself before he gave her the ammunition to hurt him any further.

She ate some of the casserole, but without any enthusiasm because she was worried now.

Worried that she might still lose the baby, which Marco seemed to think was a possibility.

Worried that she'd got her parents all excited, and then might have to snatch that happiness away.

Worried also that for some reason she'd lost the closeness she and Marco had had today at the hospital, because it seemed that somehow she had, but she didn't know why or how.

Why was he so cross that she'd told her parents? Or maybe he wasn't cross, but he was certainly something. Distant, at the very least, but only since her phone call and it had been like throwing a switch. Anyone would think she'd told *his* parents, but she wouldn't ever do that because it wasn't her place to tell them and, anyway, he had enough problems with them, by all accounts. But surely she could tell her own parents whatever she liked? Even if it *was* a little too soon, under the circumstances…

She pushed her plate away, barely touched, and gathered her things together. She had a sudden and desperate need to be back in her own home, not his, because she was done dreaming about happy ever after and letting herself get carried away with roses and lavender and ridiculous nonsense when she had no idea what he really felt or wanted.

She knew what she wanted—her life back on an even keel, without this emotional wringer she was putting herself through with Marco.

She didn't need him, she could do this alone. She was happy—more than happy—for him to be part of the baby's life, if there still was a baby in the end, but she didn't need him in hers, not if it meant this endless turmoil. She'd be fine. Really. Why not? Lots of women did it on their own.

She swiped away the tears that she hadn't even known were falling, and sitting down at the breakfast bar she scrawled a note.

Gone home, feeling much better. Thank you for looking after me. I'm fine now.
A

She hesitated, then didn't put an *x*, just left the note on the worktop where he'd find it, but as she got to her feet she heard the scrape of a key in the lock and Marco walked in.

He looked at her, looked at the coat over her arm and the note on the worktop and frowned.

'Where are you going?'

'Home. I thought I'd cluttered up your life enough today,' she said, and he swore softly and walked up to her, tilting her face up so he could see the tears that were welling again, to her disgust.

'Oh, Alice,' he murmured, and wiped them away with a gentle stroke of his thumbs. 'I'm sorry. I shouldn't have said that about the baby—'

'No, you're right, it is a possibility, and maybe it was too soon to tell my parents, but you didn't need to be so angry about it—'

'I wasn't angry!'

'Well, it certainly felt like it from where I was standing.'

He shook his head slowly, his eyes puzzled. 'No. I was never angry. Hurt, maybe. I thought we were getting somewhere today, getting closer, and then...'

'Then you heard me tell my mother we were just friends,' she said, realising what it was about the phone call that had upset him. Of course...

'*Colleagues*,' he said bluntly. 'How could you do that, Alice? How could you dismiss how close we were today?' He let out his breath on a soft huff and looked away. 'I was going to talk to you about us, about our relationship, see what we could build together so we have a strong foundation before the baby comes.'

He looked back at her, his eyes weary now. 'At the very least I thought we could be friends—good friends, close friends. Maybe more—much more. I know it's too soon to talk about what form the future's going to take for us, but we will have one, Alice, we'll have to, for the baby's sake, and maybe even for ours. We have to work towards that, and we have to do it together. I can't do it alone.'

She stared at him, feeling like her strings had been cut, and all the hurt and anger and worry drained away and left her exhausted and confused.

'I thought—I don't know what I thought. Marco, I'm sorry, I didn't mean to hurt you. It's just been a really difficult day, and I can't think straight. I need to go to bed, I'm so tired.'

'Then stay here, with me. At least for tonight.'

'I can't. It's not fair on you—'

He cupped her shoulders gently. 'What's not

fair on me? Alice, I *want* you to stay. Let me look after you, please? You had a threatened miscarriage today and it brought it home to me how much I want our baby, how much I want to be part of its life, and part of yours. I don't know on what basis, but I do want to be part of it. Don't shut the door on that, Alice, please. There's far too much at stake.'

She stared up into his face, trying to read his eyes, but the light was behind him. 'You want to be part of my life?'

'Yes. Definitely. I will be, whatever happens. And who knows? We may end up together, we may not. I hope we do, but it's too soon yet, we need time before we can say that for sure. The last thing we need is to leap into marriage and end up with a hideous divorce and the baby caught in the middle. That's what could have happened with Francesca, and I won't let it happen to us. We need to take it steady, wait until we're sure. And in the meantime, you need to let me look after you, especially today.'

She gave a shaky sigh and rested her head against his chest, and he gathered her into his arms and held her, his thumb stroking her back rhythmically.

'I didn't mean it,' she said, and then tilted her head back so he could see her. 'About us just being colleagues. I was just trying to defuse the situation, because I didn't want my mother to start jumping to conclusions and telling all her friends there was going to be a wedding—and my phone hasn't stopped ringing. I've had to turn it off because my brothers have all been on the phone trying to talk to me and I just don't want to talk to them yet. I wish I hadn't told her—'

'No, you should have. She's your mother, Alice. A woman needs her mother at this time, it's what happens, all part of being a family. I'd like to meet them.'

'Would you?' She rested her head against his chest again. 'Be careful what you wish for, Marco. They can be pretty full-on.'

She heard the low chuckle deep in his chest. 'Oh, Alice. I have seven siblings to your three. Don't tell me about full-on. I know exactly how it is.' He eased away from her and turned her towards the sitting room. 'Come and sit down and put your feet up—unless you want to go to bed already? That's fine with me.'

She tipped her head on one side and smiled at him wryly. 'I don't believe I've said I'll stay,' she murmured, but he just smiled back.

'You didn't need to. So what's it to be? Sofa or bed?'

'Bed, I think—but I haven't got any things here.'

'Yes, you have. Your hospital bag was still in my car. I've brought it in.'

'You have? Wasn't that jumping the gun a bit?'

His smile had some of the old familiar Marco in it. 'I can be very persuasive,' he said softly, and she chuckled tiredly.

'Come on, then, show me where I'm sleeping.'

They went upstairs, and to her surprise he pushed open his bedroom door.

'Oh. Your room?'

'Why not? My bed's the size of a football pitch, and I won't intrude on your privacy, if that's what you're worrying about, but I do want to be near you, just in case. Or I can sleep next door if you really want me to, but this way you have the en suite bathroom, and it's more comfortable.'

She hesitated, but his bed looked so inviting, and there was a gorgeous view of the sunset through the floor-length windows. She could lie in bed and watch it set, and it might be nice to have him near...

She told him so, and he hugged her gently.

'Thank you. I'll be much happier near you, too. Did you eat any of that casserole?'

She shook her head. 'Only a little. I didn't feel hungry—too wound up, I think.'

'Maybe later. You have a nap now, and call me if you want anything. I'll just be in my study up here and I'll leave the door open. The bathroom's through here.'

He pushed open a door she hadn't even noticed, and she nodded and turned to him with a smile.

'Thank you, Marco.'

'What, for pointing out the bathroom?'

She laughed, then her smile faded and she reached up and touched his face. 'No. For everything. For looking after me, for being there for me today when it could have all gone hideously wrong, for standing by me, for wanting to share my life—for all of it, really.'

He stared at her for a long time, then his face softened into a tender smile.

'Oh, Alice. Come here.'

He pulled her gently into his arms, held her for a long, lingering moment and then let her go. 'Go on, get ready for bed. I'll make you a drink. Peppermint tea?'

She shook her head. 'Just hot water would be lovely. Thank you.'

He closed the door, and she undressed and pulled on her pyjamas and crawled into his bed—not the side with the book and clock on the bedside table, because that was obviously where he usually slept, but the other side, furthest from the door.

She'd meant to watch the sunset, but as she snuggled down between sheets made of the softest cotton and breathed in the scent of him, it was as if she was cradled in his arms, and she drifted off to sleep in seconds, the sunset forgotten.

She'd gone to sleep.

He stood and stared down at her, the paleness of her hair against his pillow, and she looked so right there he felt a lump in his throat.

Did they stand a chance? *Dio,* he hoped so, because bit by tiny bit she was edging into his heart and carving out her own little niche.

He went back down to the kitchen, put the casserole into the fridge and made a heap of pasta with pesto, grated a ton of *parmigiano* cheese over it and ate it at his desk with a fork while he sat and worked his way through his emails. Then he used the other bathroom, turned off all the lights except the one on the landing, and slid quietly into bed beside her.

For a while he lay there watching her sleep and wondering where their relationship was going, and then he gave up trying to second-guess the future and closed his eyes, content to listen to the soft sound of her breathing as his body relaxed and sleep claimed him, too.

He woke her with a kiss, and she hauled herself out of a beautiful dream and realised it wasn't a dream at all, she really was in his bed. Had she spent the night in his arms? Maybe…

'Morning, *tesoro*,' he murmured. 'How are you?'

'I'm OK,' she said, realising she was. 'I feel much better.'

'Good. I've put you some hot water and crackers here, and there's an avocado and some eggs on the side in the kitchen. I have to go. I've got a day-case list at nine and I've got a ton of stuff to do before then.'

'What time is it?'

'Only half past six. I'll see you later. Don't rush,' he said, and stooped and kissed her again, just a fleeting touch of his lips before he left, but it left a warm feeling inside her, and she found herself smiling.

She didn't dawdle, because she had a lot to do herself, but she sipped the hot water and ate a couple of crackers before she headed for the bathroom. She had a quick shower without washing her hair because she had no idea if he had a hairdryer, then went down to the kitchen, made some breakfast and walked home to pick up her car.

By the time she arrived at the hospital he was already occupied with pre-op checks on his day-case patients, so she did a quick ward round to see how her patients were.

Daisy and Amil were side by side in the ward now, and Alice was pleased to see that they were eating at last. Tiny amounts, carefully controlled and still supplemented by the TPN drip, but a huge improvement on five or six days ago.

There was no sign of either set of parents, though, which troubled her.

'Are you OK to be at work?'

She turned at the softly murmured words and met Marco's searching eyes.

'Yes. I'm fine.'

'Sure?'

She nodded. 'Perfectly. I wouldn't be here if I wasn't, I'm not silly.'

He gave a nod and walked off, and she finished what she was doing and went back down to Reception. Maybe Olive was in the café, having breakfast?

She was, and Alice walked over to her with a smile.

'Mind if I join you?'

'No, not at all.' She pulled her coffee towards her, and Alice felt a little wave of revulsion.

Too late. She sat down, put it out of her mind and concentrated on the core business.

'I'm sorry I haven't been around over the weekend. How do you feel Daisy's been?'

'Much better. She seems a lot more comfortable. I've spent quite a bit of time with her, and Dan came in yesterday so I took the chance to go home and do some washing and have a bit of a tidy up.'

'How's he coping?' she asked, and Olive shrugged.

'I don't know. We don't really talk about it. He comes, he stays a while, he leaves. I don't think he's enjoying it, but that's not what it's about, is it? But at least he's making the effort.'

'He does find it hard, doesn't he?'

Olive sighed and stirred her coffee, sending another wave of the aroma towards Alice. 'Yes, he does. I won't lie to you, things aren't great between us, but since her operation he's not really talked much at all. Men are like that, aren't they? Trying to understand them is all guesswork, and I think a lot of the time I get it wrong.'

Oh, how true. She thought of her conversation with Marco after she'd talked to her parents, and she smiled. 'At least he's trying now. And she's getting better steadily, so hopefully that'll continue and you'll be able to take her home soon without any more symptoms. That's what we're aiming for, that she should be able to live a normal life and you won't have to worry about her being in pain whenever she eats.'

'Oh, I hope so. Maybe then he'll want to spend more time with us—maybe even have another child. Who knows? I haven't dared think about it because of Daisy needing so much of my attention, but—maybe now? I don't know, though. Dan might not want it. He might just be waiting for Daisy to be better before he leaves me.'

'Really?' That shocked her. 'Do you think that's a possibility, Olive?'

'I don't know. I hope not, because I do still love him, but he's got so distant...'

Like Marco, tenderness one minute, distant the next—only he hadn't been, not really, and all it had taken was a simple conversation to sort it out.

'I think you need to talk.'

'We do, but I'm putting it off because I'm afraid of the answer,' Olive confessed. 'At least this way I can pretend.'

'I don't think it's fooling Daisy,' she said gently, reaching out and touching Olive's hand.

'I know. I need to talk to him, because I can't live like this and it's cruel to leave her with so many doubts. It's just finding a way.'

Alice squeezed Olive's hand. 'I hope you can find it, and I hope it goes well. I'm always around if you need to talk.'

She got up with a smile, and left Olive to finish her coffee while she headed up to her office to check on her day's schedule. It wasn't quite eight, but she knew they had a busy week ahead and she didn't want Marco to feel he had to manage all of it alone.

Assuming the baby stayed where it was and everything continued to settle down. She had her follow-up on Thursday, to check the hormone levels in her blood hadn't fallen and that everything was resolving. Would he want to come?

Yes, of course. He'd been there for her yesterday, every inch of the way.

She put it out of her mind, went into her office, turned on her computer and while it was booting up she checked her phone, and there was a message from Marco.

I thought you might want this. M x

He'd attached the video of the scan, and she saved it without playing it. Time enough for that when she was at home. For now, she had other priorities, none of which involved listening to her baby's heartbeat.

* * *

She ran into him later, while she was on her lunch break, and her heart gave a curious little thump.

'I thought you were in Theatre?'

He shook his head. 'I've done my list. Everyone's in Recovery or back on the ward. How about you? You seem to be hanging around without a job. Why don't you go home? You should be resting.'

'Marco, I'm fine. I've done my outpatients, done my admin, checked on Daisy and Amil, spoken to both sets of parents—well, more or less. I spoke to Olive.'

His brow creased. 'Ah. I was going to talk to you about them. Dan doesn't seem to be around. He was here yesterday, but not for that long, and she'd gone home, so I spent some time with Daisy just having a chat.'

'And?' she asked, because she could see there was more.

'And she's not happy. She thinks they're both sad, and it's making her sad. Oh, and Alana's coming tomorrow. I thought she could see Daisy and Amil, if you're OK with that? It might cheer them both up.'

'Yes, of course. I think it's a great idea.'

'Good. I'll send her an email confirming. And go home. I've got this.'

He made an expansive gesture to indicate the hospital, and to be fair to him she *was* tired.

'OK. But just today—just in case…'

He nodded his understanding, and his expression softened.

'Call me if you need to.'

She didn't.

Need to, or call him.

She cooked herself something nutritious and relatively odourless for supper, had an early night and was fine the next day. Whatever had happened at the weekend seemed to be behind her, and her follow-up at the end of Thursday would answer any further questions, so she put it out of her mind for now, and got on with her job.

It involved the monthly meeting of the clinical leads, another pile of letters to write, and a batch of cases to consider, and she called Marco in to discuss them and they decided who would be the best placed to operate on them.

Some were allocated to her, some—mostly the day cases—to him, and others would need their joint expertise.

And it kept her busy enough to take her mind off the baby. For now.

The hospital was filled with excitement when she went in the next morning, because it was

Halloween and there were pumpkins with battery-powered tea lights lining the entrance to the hospital, and a stall in the foyer selling fairy cakes with black and orange icing.

There was more Halloween stuff around the entrance to the ward, pumpkin-shaped cut-outs stuck to the windows, and the children who were well enough were planning a 'Trick or Treat' raid on all the staff.

Tough for the children like Daisy and Amil who weren't allowed sweets, but to Alice's surprise—or not, really, knowing her as she did—Evie had made all the children like Daisy and Amil a plaited bracelet of black and orange bands. But it didn't matter about the sweets in the end, because the kitchen staff had excelled themselves.

The children's lunches were a feast of ghostly delights—even Daisy and Amil could have some of the things they'd prepared, and lunchtime was an adventure.

And then of course there was Marco dressed as Count Dracula, with fake blood running down his chin and surgical gloves with paper talons stuck on the end.

'Don't you have anything useful to do today?' she asked, but he just laughed.

'Yes. Of course. But this is just as important.'

'As operating?'

'You can talk.'

'I'm on my lunch break,' she pointed out.

'What, eating the kids' mock pumpkins and googly eyeballs?'

'What's wrong with that? Eyeballs are highly nutritious.'

He snorted softly, then shook his head. 'I need to get on. I have kids to scare.'

'Yeah, right,' she said, because there was nothing scary about Marco and they all knew it.

But he winked at her, bared his fangs and wandered off, and she turned away and swallowed a sudden lump in her throat, because he was going to make a brilliant father for their baby, and he'd be an amazing life partner—if only it all worked out.

CHAPTER SEVEN

'YOU HAVE TO see this.'

Alice looked up from her desk. 'See what? I'm writing a discharge letter.'

'Daisy and Doodle. And Wuzzle.'

Wuzzle? She got up, trying to stifle her smile. 'I meant to ask—how is Wuzzle?'

His mouth softened into a grin. 'He's much better, thank you. He had his stitches out this morning.'

She felt her mouth twitch. 'Did he?'

'Yes, he did. And he's telling Doodle all about it.'

He was. Daisy was sitting propped up in bed, Alana in a chair on one side of her, and Doodle, the soppy great thing, was lying on Daisy's bed staring attentively up at her and Wuzzle as she talked, his tail waving softly.

'And now I'm *all* better,' Daisy said in a high, squeaky voice, and then giggled.

Doodle's plume of a tail waved a bit harder,

and he rested his head on Daisy's thigh and sighed, his eyes still fixed on her face.

'Oh, Wuzzle. I think Doodle's tired, don't you?' she said, and the tail waved again. She tucked Wuzzle in between Doodle's paws, and Doodle looked down at him, rested his head beside Wuzzle and sighed again.

Alice heard a soft click, and realised Marco had taken a photo. 'For Olive,' he said softly, and she nodded.

'She'll like that.'

Daisy heard their voices and looked up. 'Wuzzle and Doodle have made friends,' she said, her face brighter than Alice had ever seen it.

'That's lovely. Doodle's very nice, isn't he? And I hear Wuzzle's all better now.'

'He is—and I'm nearly all better. I had toast this morning.'

'Did you? And were you all right?'

She nodded. 'Yes. It was very nice. It had chocolate spread on it, but not much. Jenny said I could only have a little bit. And then I had some chicken and rice for lunch, and ice cream. It was yummy.'

'That's great news, Daisy,' Alice said, glad that Jenny, the nurse assigned to Daisy, had managed to find something that the little girl dared to eat. She'd become afraid of food because it had caused her pain in the past, and it was a relief to know that she was starting to enjoy it again.

Alana looked at her watch and got to her feet. 'Right, Daisy, I think Doodle and I have to go and see another little girl somewhere else, but I'll come again tomorrow, if you like?'

Daisy nodded enthusiastically, and gave Doodle a lovely gentle cuddle before he hopped off the bed, had a little shake and trotted off by Alana's side.

'Do you know where Mummy is?' Daisy asked, but Alice shook her head.

'No, I don't. Marco?'

He shook his head. 'No, but I'll call her, *bellissima*. Don't worry, she'll be here soon.'

'Where's Amil?'

'He's gone to have some pictures taken of his insides. He shouldn't be long. And I'll come back soon, I promise.'

They walked away together, and Alice gave him a searching look. 'Pictures?' she said, and he nodded.

'Yes, a follow-through contrast scan, and also a lactose intolerance test. But now I need to send this picture to Olive and find out where the hell they are.'

His mouth was set in a grim line, and Alice knew he was tamping down his anger at the couple, although Olive was almost always at Daisy's side.

'I've got my follow-up appointment in an hour,' she murmured, and his eyes snapped up to hers.

'I know.'

'Did you want to come?'

'Yes. Can I? I don't know.'

'Don't worry if you can't.'

'I can,' he said decisively. 'I'll come back later if necessary. Let me have a quick word with Jenny, and I'll be back with you. Don't go without me.'

They had a longer wait this time, but the scan showed the baby's heart was still beating strongly and her blood pressure was down, which was all good news, so the nurse took some blood for comparison of the pregnancy hormone levels.

'We'll get the results back to you in the next day or so,' the nurse she'd seen before told her, 'and in the meantime if there's any more bleeding or you're worried about anything, just call us, but so far it's looking positive so we're hopeful.'

So was Alice, but Marco seemed preoccupied. It was only after they'd returned to the car and he was heading back to the hospital that he spoke.

'So, that's good news.'

'It is. It's looking more and more likely that we're going to have a baby, so I'm glad I told my parents. Are you still cross about that?'

He frowned. 'I'm not cross, Alice. I thought maybe it was a bit hasty, under the circumstances, but only because I was worried. Anyway, you seem to be all right now, which is good, but I don't think we should tell my parents yet, because I don't want either of us put under that much pressure. If you think your mother's over-eager to get you married and settled down, wait till you meet mine.'

Which she would, of course, in just over a week. 'Marco, do you think I should go to the wedding? Do you think it'll be safe for me to fly?'

He frowned. 'I don't know. It's a good point. If you've only had a very little spotting, and it's finished, and the baby's looking fine and your hormone levels are good and nothing else changes, I don't see why not, but if you'd rather we could drive—although that would probably be more tiring for you.'

She nodded. 'It's a long way to Italy.'

'Not that far. Well, it is, it's just over a thousand miles. I have driven it, but not just for the weekend. It takes about sixteen or seventeen hours non-stop.'

'Do you do it in one?'

'I have done. Another option is the train, but that's twelve hours at the least, so again a lot of sitting. Flying is certainly the fastest and least tiring way.'

She nodded. 'Can I see how I feel nearer the time?'

'Sure. I don't want you to go if you're not happy with it. I heard from Olive, by the way,' he added grimly. 'She and Dan were "talking", as she put it. She didn't sound happy.'

Alice dropped her head back against the headrest and sighed. 'Oh, no. I was afraid it might come to this. I have a horrible feeling they're heading for divorce, from what she said on Monday.'

'Well, I hope not, for Daisy's sake. I want to shake that man.'

'Get in the queue,' she said drily as he turned into the hospital and parked the car. 'Are you going back in?'

'Yes, I have work to do. All that time prancing around as Count Dracula yesterday, as you would say.'

She laughed softly. 'I didn't say a word.'

'You didn't need to.' He turned his head and

searched her eyes in the gloom. 'What are you doing about eating this evening?'

'I don't know. Nothing yet. I need to go shopping.'

'I have food in my fridge.'

She hesitated, probably for too long because he shrugged.

'It was just an idea, but I might be a bit late anyway. Don't worry if you'd rather not,' he said, which made it sound as if he was regretting asking her, so she let him off the hook.

'Actually, I'd probably be better buying some food, cooking something simple fairly soon and having an early night, but thank you for the offer. And thank you for taking me to the hospital.'

'You're welcome.'

She reached for the door handle but he stopped her with a hand on her shoulder.

'I'm glad it was good news about the baby,' he said softly. 'I've been worrying about you both.'

She turned back and smiled at him. 'I know you have, and I have, too, but it looks like we can stop worrying now. Don't work too late.'

And with that she got out of the car and walked towards her own, and she heard him close his door, heard the plink of the central locking as he walked away.

'*Ciao, bellissima,*' he said over his shoulder. 'See you tomorrow. Sleep well.'

'Goodnight, Marco. Thanks again.'

He lifted his hand but kept walking, and she suddenly felt ridiculously alone. Why had she turned down his invitation? What did it matter if he was late? She could have had a nap and gone round later, done a bit more towards working at this relationship that they were going to need instead of saying no yet again. Was that any way to get closer to him?

She got into her car, dropped her head down on the steering wheel and gave a stifled scream, then wondered how Olive and Dan were getting on.

Not well, judging by the sound of it. Why were relationships so difficult?

Her follow-up results gave her the all clear on Monday, and she phoned them and asked about flying and was told she was probably at no more risk than she would have been without the very minor bleed, but that it had to be her decision.

They didn't say *don't*, which in a way she'd been hoping for.

An excuse to get out of the wedding? Probably.

Still, there was the rest of the week to get

through before then, and her first and most pressing problem was Daisy.

She was refusing to eat again, and there was little sign of Dan, either.

And then things came to a head when Marco walked into the room, his face like thunder.

'Can I have a word?'

'Sure.' She pushed back her chair and turned to face him. 'What's wrong?

'Daisy. The Christmas trees have been put up, and the kids are all talking about writing letters to Santa. I said it was a bit early, but Daisy wanted me to help her write hers, so she told me what she wanted to say and I put the dots for the letters and she wrote over them.'

'And?' she asked, because there was obviously an 'and'.

'She asked Santa to make her mummy and daddy happy again.'

She felt her chest clench. 'Oh, Marco. That's so sad.'

'I know. I struggled a bit,' he said, and his eyes were glittering now with unshed tears. 'She's been so brave, and she's just run out of being able to cope. And Alana told me she told Doodle that she thinks her daddy doesn't love her any more.'

'Oh, no! Oh, Marco, that's dreadful! Oh, *poor* little Daisy.'

She felt her eyes fill, and she looked away, sniffing hard.

'Here.'

He was holding out a tissue, and she grabbed it and blew her nose. 'Sorry. That just got to me.'

'Don't worry. It got to me, too. At least you can blame it on your hormones. I just wanted to hit something, so I hit the wall. Better than Dan, but still not a good idea.'

It wasn't. She could see the bruise coming out on the side of his hand, and she didn't fancy the wall's chances, either.

'You need to take care of your hands. You can't work with broken fingers.'

'Tell me about it. Don't worry, they're not broken, they're just bruised. I've iced them and put arnica and ibuprofen gel on.'

'Well, at least it wasn't Dan.'

'No. That's why I'm talking to you, because someone has to address this and I don't think it should be me. I wouldn't trust myself.'

She sighed. 'Do you know if they're around today?'

'Olive is. She wasn't there when Daisy told Doodle that, she'd gone to get a coffee, otherwise I don't think Daisy would have said it. Will you talk to them?'

She nodded. 'Yes, of course I will. I'll have

to ask Olive if she can contact Dan and get him to come in. I don't have his contact details. He seemed reluctant to leave them.'

'I wonder why,' Marco said drily, and opened the door. 'Let me know how it goes.'

As expected, was the answer to that.

She called them both into her office later that afternoon, closed the door and turned to them.

'We're worried about Daisy. She's stopped eating again, and we don't think it's because she's sore.' She hesitated, then went on, 'I realise things are difficult with you both, and I don't wish to interfere, but you should know that Daisy's dictated a letter to Santa, the gist of which is that she wants you all to be a happy family again, and she told Doodle, the therapy dog, that she doesn't think you love her any more, Dan.'

Dan sucked in his breath, his face racked with guilt and grief, and Alice felt a pang of regret for having to tell them. 'I'm sorry. I know that's hard to take, but I didn't feel we could sit on it. Perhaps I can leave it with you?'

They nodded, and Alice could see that Dan was on the verge of tears.

'Why don't you stay here for a little while? I'll put the engaged sign on the door, and you can stay for as long as you want. Or, if you've still got a family suite, you could take yourselves up there and make a cup of tea and sit and chat. That might be better.'

They nodded again, both of them seemingly bereft of words, and Alice squeezed Olive's shoulder and ushered them out, watching them go with a heavy heart.

'How was it?' Marco asked softly, coming up behind her.

'Grim. He looked gutted.'

'I expect he was. He's her father, after all. He can't feel nothing for her, even if that's what comes over.'

'So why did you want to hit him?'

'I didn't. That's why I hit the wall.'

They both looked down at his hand, and she frowned and picked it up and looked at it, turning it over, prodding it gently.

'Ouch.'

'Sorry. Marco, are you sure you haven't got a fracture?'

'Not entirely, but I'll live. It'll make me more circumspect in future.'

She laughed at that. 'I doubt it. Will you be able to operate tomorrow?'

'I don't know. I'll tell you when I find out. We've got another complex case coming in, so I hope so. Can we discuss it?'

* * *

He was an idiot.

He knew that, but the following day he had a baby with gastro-oesophageal reflux disease who was coming in for repair to his diaphragm and a fundoplication, using the top of the stomach to strengthen the sphincter at the base of the oesophagus. And he would need both hands in good working order to do it, or else he'd have to ask Alice, which he didn't want to do. Not after he'd been such an idiot.

He didn't really know why he'd hit the wall. Because he was mad with Dan? Or because he was mad with himself, because he'd allowed himself to get so emotionally involved with Alice and the child she was carrying? Their baby. His baby, her baby. And he might end up like Dan, marginalised in the child's affections, pushed out by the failure of an already fragile relationship with its mother, so that the baby ended up losing that closeness with both parents that was every child's birthright.

Or should be.

His father had withdrawn from him when he'd told him he was going into medicine and not the family business. Not physically, because they had still been living in the same house, eating in the same room, sharing the space. But the closeness between father and son had gone, and it had never come back.

And that *hurt. Dio*, how it hurt. It had hurt him then, and it still hurt him now, sixteen, seventeen years later. Almost half his life.

So he knew how little Daisy felt, and he was desperate that his own child would *never* feel that pain, and to ensure that he would have to focus harder on his relationship with Alice and make it work. But how?

He would have to woo her. He hadn't really done it, he realised, hadn't pulled out all the stops and done his best to convince her that they should be together, partly because he'd concentrated on making sure she and the baby were all right rather than exploring their own relationship. And it hadn't been enough to gain her trust, he realised, remembering how hurt she must have been by her previous relationship.

More hurt than he'd appreciated when she'd told him? Probably, because every time he made an approach, every time he kissed her or offered to feed her, she either gave in with slight reluctance or pulled away, but always he could sense this fight in her, the need to keep herself apart from him as if she daren't trust him completely.

And he wanted her to trust him, wanted her to

feel that he would never do anything to hurt her. He wanted her to get to know him, wanted to get to know her—the real her, not the façade that she put on to protect herself, convince everyone that she was fine, that she didn't need anything or anyone, which was blatantly not true.

They had the wedding—assuming that she was still all right, which looked probable. He would whisk her away, lavish affection on her, spoil her, pamper her—make love to her, maybe, in the way he should have done in the one chance he'd had, only he'd blown it.

Well, not this time.

This time, he'd make sure she knew just how much he cared, just how much he wanted her. Because he did want her, the crazy, stubborn, complicated woman that she was, and not just for the baby.

He wanted Alice Baxter for herself, and he was going to have to up his game if he was going to stand a chance of getting her. But in the meantime he'd take the pressure off, stop cornering her for a kiss, bribing her with food and all the other things he'd been doing, because they clearly weren't working and might even be doing the opposite. No, he'd stand back for a little while and let Alice make the first move. If she did. And then at least he might know where he stood.

* * *

To her huge relief, Olive and Dan seemed to have come to an understanding, and over the next few days Daisy started eating again, but only a tiny bit. Gradually, though, she was increasing the amount, and for the first time since it had all blown up, Alice felt that Daisy was now stable enough that she might be able to go away at the weekend for the wedding with Marco.

And if the worst came to the worst, the hospital was staffed with excellent surgeons, many of whom could take over. Theo Hawkwood, for a start, although he was more and more preoccupied with Ivy.

Alice had lost count of the number of tests Ivy was supposed to have had, and there had been multi-disciplinary meetings with anyone who had anything to offer being asked to attend and discuss her case.

Madison Archer, the American diagnostician Theo had taken on, had finally arrived and was slowly and methodically working through all the test results, and Theo was pinning his hopes on her.

Poor Theo. He'd been haunting the hospital, spending most of his time either engaged in research or sleeping at Ivy's bedside, and so far they'd all come up with nothing.

She pitied Madison. That was a lot of responsibility, and a huge weight on her shoulders, brilliant though she might be.

Still, nothing Alice could do, it was way out of her field and Marco's so they hadn't been involved in the MDT meetings, but it seemed as if nothing much apart from decorating the hospital for Christmas was going to happen in the next week if the buzz in the wards was to be believed.

Starting with the huge Christmas trees Evie had ordered all the way from Scandinavia. They'd arrived on Friday morning, and by the time she left the hospital that evening they were safely up and held in place by guy ropes, and a cherry picker had arrived in time for the trees to be decorated over the weekend.

Not that they'd be there, because it was the weekend of the wedding and they'd be in Italy.

Her heart thumped, and she felt a quiver of unease. What would his family make of her? She'd have to shore up her defences and make certain she didn't give away anything that she felt for Marco in front of his family.

Or in front of him, come to that, because for the last week he hadn't asked her to eat with him, offered to cook for her—he wasn't being unfriendly, and their working relationship was fine, but it was as if in some way he'd withdrawn from her, and she felt it like a cold draught around her heart.

She packed on Friday night as soon as she got home, because they were leaving first thing in the morning. Marco was picking her up at seven in a taxi and they were taking the train to Stansted and flying into Pisa, and she managed to get everything she'd need into a cabin bag.

Well, she hoped it was everything. A simple LBD that wouldn't crease for the dinner on Saturday, the blue dress she'd worn for the gala— complete with tiny plucks which she'd pulled through to the other side and didn't show—and a jacket to cover it for the ceremony, one pair of heels and some ballet flats. Minimal toiletries and make-up, thin pyjamas, changes of underwear and the clothes she stood up in. Her passport, purse and phone were in the neat little clutch she'd use for the wedding, and there was room for it to fit in her case.

That would do. It wasn't as if she was an important guest.

She was at the door when the taxi pulled up outside, and she was halfway down the path with her bag when he took it from her and told her off for carrying it.

'It doesn't weigh anything, Marco,' she said, but he just arched a brow.

'Where's the rest?'

'There is no rest. That's it.'

His eyebrow climbed into his hair, and he blew out his breath and shook his head. 'If you say so.'

He handed it to the taxi driver, held the door for her and got in on the other side, and they pulled away.

'OK?'

She nodded, although she wasn't sure. The butterflies were having a field day in her stomach at the prospect of meeting his family, and she just hoped her breakfast would stay put.

She looked—no, not nervous. A little uncertain?

He was waiting all the way to the airport for her to say she'd left something vital behind, but she didn't, and although she looked a little pale on take-off and landing, the flight was smooth and mercifully short and they were out of passport control in record time.

'So, welcome to Italy,' he said with a smile as their feet hit the paving outside the airport building just four and a half hours after he'd picked her up. 'Now we need the car.'

He rang the number, and two minutes later a car glided to a halt outside the front of the airport terminal. He loaded the luggage, tipped the driver and got behind the wheel.

'That was easy,' she said, sounding surprised, but he just grinned.

'I've used the firm before. They're good.'

'I thought you didn't come home?'

'I don't—not often—but I've been to the odd wedding and I've met up with Raffaello and Gio a couple of times.'

'Are they the ones you're closest to?'

He nodded. 'Not in age, maybe, but in other ways. You'll meet them soon.'

'Are we going straight to your home?' she asked, and he nodded.

'Yes. We'll be there in time for lunch—unless you'd rather go somewhere else on the way? How are you feeling?'

'OK. I could probably do with eating something fairly soon.'

'So—food first?'

'Please.'

'OK.'

He pulled out of the airport, up the ramp onto the main road and headed south east towards home. There was a trattoria in a little hill town just off the road which he'd used before. It was full of charm, had a lovely view across the valley and served good, honest Italian food, and it would be perfect.

* * *

Alice settled back against the comfortable leather seat of the obviously expensive hire car. Strange, that he'd hired a car like this and yet they'd flown with a budget airline. Because it was the most direct route? It certainly hadn't taken long, and the seats had been fine for her, although she thought Marco would have been a bit cramped. But then he didn't really do ostentatious. So—why the car? To impress his family?

No. He'd given up doing that years ago. To impress her, then? He ought to know she wasn't impressed by things like that.

'Are you OK? Is the seat comfortable?'

'It's lovely—it's great.'

'I was hoping it would be. The country roads are a bit rough in places, especially where we're going, and I didn't want you to be jostled about.'

Well, that answered that question, and not at all in the way she'd expected. He was doing what he always did, looking after her, and she was too busy looking for ulterior motives to realise it. How stupid of her. It was time she learned to trust him.

'I'm not jostled at all. It's lovely. Thank you.'

'You're welcome.'

She rested her head back and studied her surroundings. As they left the city outskirts the

buildings gradually gave way to open countryside, a chequerboard of neat fields interspersed
with avenues of Lombardy poplars snaking
along the valley bottom and climbing the hills
at each side.

Some of the fields had olive trees planted
in them with geometric precision, others had
vines, gnarled and twisted, the leaves in glorious autumn colours.

It was a beautifully sunny day, and as they
left the valley bottom and climbed through an
avenue of poplars to a small cluster of buildings
perched on a hill-top, she could see for miles.

'It's beautiful,' she said softly, and he reached
out and took her hand and squeezed it.

'It is. I'm glad you can see that. I love it.'

'Maybe you should come back more often.'

He flashed her a smile. 'Maybe I should.
Maybe we should. We'll see. Right, let's get
lunch.'

They left the little hill town an hour later after
a light but delicious meal, and headed back
down to the valley bottom, picking up the main
road again for half an hour until he turned off
through huge stone gateposts with a pretty gate
lodge at one side.

'Here we are. Castello di Ricci, the seat of the
family empire,' he said drily, and as they headed

along the neat gravel drive she noticed his face had fallen into that set, unreadable expression she was all too familiar with.

She reached out and laid her hand over his on the steering wheel. 'Hey. It'll be OK.'

He flashed her a smile. 'Yeah. It will. Are you OK?'

She nodded, not entirely sure, but she wasn't going to do anything to make his life more awkward and she could see he definitely had mixed feelings.

Would his family greet him coolly? She hoped not. The thought of her family being anything other than delighted to see her was chilling. Did he face that every time?

Apparently not.

They pulled up in a gravelled courtyard at the foot of a broad sweep of steps that rose to a massive door, and as she got out of the car she could see a welcoming committee at the top of the steps.

A man almost identical to Marco ran down the steps and hugged and kissed him, followed by others—a sister, maybe, who flew down the steps and hurled herself into his arms, another brother, who hugged him and slapped his back, and then his parents, his mother beaming, his father more reserved. They shook hands, but his father still hugged him, though, so clearly he didn't hate him that much.

And then they all turned their attention to her and the babble of Italian fell silent.

'This is Alice—she's a friend of mine, and she's also my boss, so please don't tell her too much about me,' he said in English with a slightly strained smile, and one by one they greeted her as he introduced them, first his mother Sofia, then his father Riccardo, his brother Gio, then Annalisa, the bride and the sister who'd thrown herself at him.

And then it was the turn of the younger man who'd been the first to reach him. He hugged her, kissed her cheeks and grinned at her. 'You're his boss? I don't envy you. Marco's never been good at doing what he's told. I'm Raffaello, by the way. It's a pleasure to meet you. Welcome to Castello di Ricci.'

CHAPTER EIGHT

ALICE WAS STUNNED by the warmth of the welcome they gave her, but she was well aware that there was a lot of curiosity mixed in with the warmth.

His boss? She'd nearly laughed at that, although technically it was true, but not in any real sense. Both hugely well qualified, they were professional equals, and it would never occur to her to tell him what to do—well, only with the admin, she thought with a smile. Professionally, at any rate, they were always on the same page.

Sofia said something to Raffaello, and he picked up her luggage, beckoned to Marco and led them up the steps and into the house.

If you could call it a house. It was huge, a cavernous entrance hall with stone stairs rising from either side, and a pair of doors leading through to a beautiful courtyard open to the elements, with a covered walkway all around the outside with doors leading off it.

She'd seen photos of it on the website Marco had shown her, but it was even more beautiful and striking in real life. They followed Raffaello through a set of doors and up a huge stone spiral staircase, the treads worn away by the passage of feet over the centuries, and halfway along a winding corridor he opened a door and ushered her in.

It was a beautiful bedroom—not huge, but with a glorious view over the valley beyond, and Raffaello opened another door and showed her the en suite shower room.

'I hope you'll be OK in here. It's not big, I'm afraid, but it should have everything you need. We'll leave you to freshen up after the journey. Marco, you're with me.'

Marco nodded, his face showing the tiniest flicker of relief, and with a promise to be back in a moment, he left the room with his brother and closed the door, and she crossed to the window and stared down into the garden.

It was beautiful. There was a rose terrace below, some of the roses still in bloom, and to the right of it a huge marquee, in readiness for the wedding tomorrow, with people bustling in and out carrying flowers and chairs and table linen.

She watched them for a moment, saw Sofia going into the marquee, presumably to supervise, and she took a step back from the window and turned to look at her room.

Everything screamed quality. It wasn't ostentatious, but it certainly wasn't cheap. She fingered the curtains, all hand-made with heavy linings, the fabric exquisite. And a glance showed that the en suite shower room was lined with honey-coloured travertine, the stone cool and smooth to the touch.

The contrast to her own family home couldn't have been much starker, and it made her acutely aware of just how out of her league he was. Her parents had struggled to fund all four of them through expensive clinical degrees, and there certainly hadn't been enough left over for luxuries. She couldn't even make a wild stab at the sum of his family's fortune, and she was sure she didn't know the half of it. What on earth did he see in her?

Although he'd always protested that the family money meant nothing to him, and he'd certainly left it all behind, even though he loved them, so maybe it really didn't matter to him.

She opened her case and shook out her clothes, hung them in the wardrobe and put her wash things in the bathroom. Not that she needed to have brought much apart from her make-up, because it was fully equipped with everything she might want, right down to a new toothbrush just in case.

Such attention to detail.

There was a tap on the door, and she opened it to find Marco standing there, hands thrust in the pockets of his jeans, his eyes warm.

'OK?' he asked, and she nodded.

'Yes. It's lovely. Come in.'

He stepped inside, closed the door and smiled at her. 'Sorry, they're a bit much. I thought I'd tell you I'm next door, through that wall.'

He jerked his thumb in the direction of the room, and she nodded. 'Sharing with your brother. Is that OK? I feel a bit guilty. You should have been in here.'

'Well, *you're* not sharing with my brother,' he said, laughter flitting through his eyes, and she smiled at that and relaxed a little.

'No. You're right, I'm not. I was a bit worried they might have put us in together.'

'No. I told my mother not to, just to avoid it. I thought it would be simpler.'

She nodded. 'Yes. It's better this way if you're trying to convince them we're just friends. Marco, can I have a guided tour? It's just occurred to me that I have no idea of the geography of this place and I don't want to get lost. You know, if I want something from my room or if there's a fire in the night.'

He frowned. 'There won't be, but if there was then you come to me and tell me. I'm not going to abandon you, Alice. You won't get lost.'

'I'd still like a guided tour,' she told him, and he smiled.

'I knew you would. That's partly why I'm here. Put a sweater on and I'll take you for a walk in the gardens, and then we can go for a drive and I'll show you the estate.'

He gave her a whistle-stop tour of the house, or the parts of it that she needed to know about, like the kitchen, the more casual sitting and dining rooms, the formal rooms they'd use tonight, the cloakrooms, and then he took her out into the garden and led her down the terrace steps and into the rose garden.

'Oh, it's so lovely,' she murmured, pausing to sniff the air. 'Just smell that. Heavenly. It must be amazing in the summer. I bet it takes a lot of looking after.'

He gave a short, wry laugh. 'Undoubtedly. I think they have several gardeners, but then there's all the grass to cut around all the holiday lets, and the shrubs and hedges to clip—it's a lot of work. Here, this is my favourite bit of the garden,' he said, leading her into the rose bower.

It was made of fine black metal hoops linked together with wires to form a semi-circular arched walkway smothered with climbing roses that made a beautiful, scented tunnel. The gravel path was sprinkled with the palest pink rose petals, adding to the romance, and she slowed to a halt and breathed in.

'Oh, Marco—it's beautiful,' she murmured, and he turned her gently into his arms.

'It is. Just made for kissing,' he replied, his voice husky to his ears.

'You know, I think you could be right,' she whispered, a slow smile playing around her mouth.

She looked up and met his eyes, and he couldn't be sure but he thought there was a yearning in them, a flicker of the real Alice. Would she pull away this time? Please, no.

He cupped her cheeks gently in his hands, bent his head and touched his lips to hers, and she sighed softly and parted them for him. He deepened the kiss, taunting, tempting her, drawing her in, and she met him touch for touch, sipping, tasting, pulling away and tracing his lips with her tongue, nipping them lightly and making him groan.

'Alice...'

Her fingers tunnelled through his hair, drawing his head down to give her better access, and he let her take the lead, driven slightly crazy by her touch. A little nip, a soothing lick, a tormenting little flick of her tongue leading to a full-on duel with his.

As if by mutual consent their hands stayed where they were, hers in his hair, his cradling her cheeks, a small gap between them that he ached to close, but he didn't. Couldn't, because at any moment someone could come along and if he touched her, if his body felt the soft, yielding pressure of hers, he'd lose what tiny fragments were left of his self-control.

Then finally she eased away and settled back on her heels, staring up at him. Her eyes were soft, almost luminous, and her lips were moist and pink and utterly irresistible—

'I think we should stop while we can,' she said, her voice unsteady. 'Someone might catch us.'

'I know,' he said wryly, and his smile felt a little out of kilter, just like his world, tilted on its axis a little bit too far, so he felt out of balance.

He lifted a hand and traced the line of her cheek, her throat, his finger pausing in the hollow at the base. He could feel the beat of her heart, steady, a little fast but slowing gradually, like his, as he came down from the enchanted high he'd shared with her.

So much for him wooing her. It seemed as if it was the other way round, but he was more than happy with that.

'We should go and find the others. I want to introduce you to my grandmother.'

He turned and she fell into step beside him. 'Tell me more about her.'

'There's nothing much to tell. She's my mother's mother, and the bedrock of my childhood, and the person I love more than anyone else in the world.'

She stopped and put her head to one side and frowned softly. 'That's not nothing, Marco.'

'No. It's not, but it's not complicated. Maybe that's what I meant by nothing much. Come, we'll go and find her.'

He bent his head and kissed her again, just lightly, and then something thudded into his thigh, and he heard a laugh as he stepped back.

'Tut, tut, Marco. Kissing the *boss* under the roses. You old romantic. Juno, come here.'

He fended the dog off with a low growl of frustration as it bounced around, and he turned to his brother with a pithy comment he really hoped Alice wouldn't understand, but his brother was still laughing and Marco looked down at Alice and kissed her again, just fleetingly, on the cheek.

'Ignore Raffe. He's an idiot.'

'I take it you don't speak Italian, Alice,' Raffaello said in English so she could understand, walking towards them with the dog now firmly glued to his side, held there by greed and the hope of the treat in his master's hand finding its way into his mouth.

'No, luckily I don't,' she said with a smile. 'Is this Juno?'

Juno wagged his tail, but his eyes were still on Raffaello and that treat. 'Yes, this is Juno. He's technically my parents' dog, but since he's slept on my bed since he was a puppy I think he qualifies as mine now. He lives with me, anyway, in my villa.'

'You don't live here?' she asked.

'No. I'm a little too old to want to live with my parents. It—uh—'

'Cramps your style?' Marco suggested drily.

'Something like that. I've been sent to find you, by the way. Mamma would like you both to join us all for an *aperitivo* before dinner.'

He nodded. 'What time and where?'

'In the *salotto* at seven. If you want anything to eat or drink before then, go and help yourselves in the kitchen. Otherwise she suggested you should just amuse yourselves because she's busy with the wedding. But you're already doing that,' he added with an impish grin that hadn't changed since his childhood.

'Thank you, Raffe. You can go now,' he said pointedly.

His brother chuckled, patted his leg to get

the dog's attention and walked away whistling softly, and Marco turned back to Alice with an apologetic smile.

'I'm sorry about that.'

'That he saw us kissing? Will he tell everyone?'

He shook his head. 'No. I've told him not to, and he of all people knows just how hard it is to keep any privacy in this family. Don't worry, it won't get out, and if it does, it might just keep my mother in check a bit and stop her introducing me to all the single women. Come on, let's go and find Nonna.'

Dinner that evening was formal but noisy, with all seven of Marco's brothers and sisters there, the older ones with their husbands and wives, and of course Marco's parents and his grandmother, his beloved *nonna* with her wise eyes and gentle smile who'd greeted Alice so sweetly a little earlier. Almost as if she'd known...

There were no children there, because tomorrow would be a long enough day for them, she guessed, but this evening was all about Annalisa, and she could feel the love of the family surrounding the young bride, the youngest of his sisters.

She found it difficult with all of them speaking Italian unless they were talking directly to her, so Marco had translated some of it and there was a vague attempt to speak in English, but she still felt a little isolated and out of the loop.

After all, she wasn't his girlfriend—he'd made that clear to everyone—and they had no idea that another Ricci grandchild was making its presence felt in subtle ways. Even so, they were lovely to her, and to Marco, and there didn't seem to be any sign of his family being angry or disappointed or distant, as he'd implied. Maybe they'd all got over it, or maybe he'd read more into it than was there, because all she could see from any of them was great affection for him, and his father's eyes hardly ever left him.

She was seated between Marco and Raffaello, which was a relief in one way, a worry in another. Could she trust him not to say something revealing about her relationship with Marco?

Yes, she realised. It was there in his eyes, the flicker of laughter dancing in them as he asked her innocently about working with his brother. 'So what's it like, being his boss?' he asked, and she laughed.

'Impossible. Do I really have to explain to you?' she said. 'He's exasperating at times, but mostly I can forgive him because he's a brilliant doctor and a highly skilled surgeon, and he's great with the little ones.'

'He's always been good with babies—he's had a lot of practice. He'll be a good father,' he added, his eyes sending her a clear message.

She felt her smile falter and looked away, unable to hold those searching, all-seeing eyes so very like his brother's. 'I'm sure he will one day,' she said, and picked up her glass, but it was empty.

'Here, have some more water,' Raffe said quietly, and she could tell just from the way that he said it that he knew. And if he knew, was it because Marco had told him, or because he'd worked it out?

She wasn't drinking alcohol, and the wine was flowing freely, so in the end she'd let someone fill her glass and taken a sip, but no more, although she lifted it to her lips a few times. Had he noticed that?

And there was a shellfish dish, which she avoided, and unpasteurised cheeses and a dessert with raw egg.

Was it obvious? She hoped not, but she was also avoiding any carbohydrates, and so hopefully anyone watching her would think she was on some ridiculous diet out of vanity and not necessity, although she wasn't sure his grandmother was fooled, either, but then maybe he'd already told her, too?

Then finally they all got to their feet and the party broke up, and Marco escorted her to her room, went in with her and gave her a long, gentle hug.

'I'm sorry, it was a bit chaotic. I thought it might be. Are you OK? Was Raffe looking after you?'

'Yes, he was. It was OK,' she lied. 'I was a bit worried they'd notice what I was eating and jump to conclusions. Had you told Raffe?'

'No, I haven't told anyone—why? Did he say something?'

'No, I just got the feeling he knew. I might be wrong.'

'I hope so. If anyone says anything I'll just tell them you're really picky and you have a medical condition that means you have to restrict certain foods as well. At least it won't be a lie.'

'I don't think pregnancy is a *medical* condition,' she pointed out wryly, but he just hugged her closer, and she rested her head on his chest and sighed.

'They're all very elegant,' she said uncertainly, wondering if she'd let him down. She'd been conscious of her simple dress all evening, but he shook his head.

'They should be, they all spend a fortune on their clothes, but I thought you looked lovely this evening. Your dress was perfect, and the dress you had for the gala is stunning. I hope you brought it?'

'Yes, I brought it. I didn't have a lot to choose from.'

'You didn't need any other choice.'

He tilted her chin, stared down into her eyes for a moment and then slowly, giving her time to back away, he kissed her.

Not like he had in the rose bower, but a simple, tender kiss, more affectionate than anything else that instead of lighting a fire inside her simply made her feel—cherished? And then he let her go, took a step back and gave her a slightly crooked smile.

'I need to go back down. My family will wonder what we're up to and we don't want to fuel the fire.'

'No. What time do I need to get up in the morning?'

'Whenever you're ready. There's plenty of time. The civil wedding's at two-thirty at the town hall, and then we'll all come back here for the religious ceremony in the *chiesa*, the little church here in the *castello*, and then we'll have drinks and canapés, and then speeches and then finally we'll sit down to dinner, which will take hours, and that'll be followed by dancing well into the night.'

'Gosh. That sounds exhausting!'

He laughed. 'It will be, but it's fun. Are you wearing heels?'

'Yes, but not too high. Not the ones I wore for the gala. I can't stand all day in them and there's usually a lot of standing around at weddings.'

'Good plan,' he said. 'Although if I know my sisters they'll kick off their shoes and dance in bare feet.'

She laughed, relieved that it wouldn't be unrelenting formality. 'I might join them.'

He smiled, told her to sleep well and knock on his door if she needed anything, and then he left her and went back to his family, and she washed and changed into her pyjamas, crawled under the covers and played the evening back in her mind.

She'd felt like an outsider—which of course she was. She got the feeling that his family didn't really understand why she was here, not if she really was just his boss, and she wasn't sure, either, apart from the obvious of meeting the family of her unborn baby, Nonna most especially. Maybe that was all he really wanted, for her to meet them and get to know them, and them her, so that when they finally broke the news it wouldn't be so totally out of the blue.

How would they react? She honestly wasn't sure. Not unlike her family, she didn't suppose. She'd had all of her brothers and their wives on the phone quizzing her endlessly, and she'd had to stop answering their calls. She guessed that was how Marco's family would be, and she could quite see why he didn't want to tell them. They'd be all over it.

She slid her hand down over her tummy, and realised there was a tiny bump. Not noticeable, she was sure, but there for all that. And suddenly it felt more real, more so even than when they'd seen the scan and heard the baby's heartbeat.

She really was going to be a mother, and he was going to be a father—the father Raffaello had said he should be.

And that, at the end of the day, was what mattered. Not his family, not her family, but her, and Marco, and their baby. And somehow, given time, she hoped they'd find a way to make it work.

The wedding was wonderful, and the weather for mid-November couldn't have been kinder.

Annalisa looked beautiful in her pure white lace gown, her tumbling rich brown hair clipped back under a long veil of incredibly delicate antique lace. Her groom, who'd met her at the doors of the little town hall, had given her a bouquet of deep red roses trailing with ivy, and when the short ceremony was over they'd been bused back to the Castello di Ricci for the church service and then they'd gathered in the enclosed courtyard for prosecco and canapés before moving to the marquee for dinner.

It wasn't like an English wedding, with a top table, but everyone was mixed up together and the bride and groom circulated between courses, bringing a lovely informality to what could have been a very stuffy occasion.

And the food was wonderful. Even though she had to be careful what she ate, to her relief Alice found there was plenty of choice, and then after the meal was finally over the tables were cleared and the dancing started.

'Come,' Marco said, his voice warm, and he led her to the dance floor and turned her into his arms.

She'd kicked off her shoes and taken off her jacket, and he laid a warm, firm hand against the bare skin of her back and eased her closer, his other hand cradling hers by her shoulder, and he rested his forehead against hers as they swayed together to the music.

This was how it had all started, she thought, him dancing with her in this dress, wearing his tux instead of the suit he wore today, but with her eyes closed it was the same, and she felt the slow burn of need start to kindle.

He shifted his head, bringing her even closer so her cheek was on his chest and his body was against hers, and she felt the change in him, felt the shift in his breathing, the heat of his breath against her skin as he groaned softly.

He wanted her. She could feel it in the tension in his muscles, hear it in the beat of his heart and the sound of his breath against her ear.

Then he lifted his head and searched her eyes, and he broke away from her slightly.

'Let's get out of here. I need some fresh air.'

They detoured back to their table to pick up her shoes and jacket, and went out into the garden, cutting across the terrace and down the steps to the rose bower.

He stopped in the middle, as he'd done the afternoon before, only this time they were bathed in the silvery light of the moon seeping through the canopy of roses as he cradled her face in his hands, his eyes glittering in the darkness. 'I want you, Alice,' he breathed, and then his mouth found hers.

This was no tender kiss, no affectionate peck or gentle graze. This was the plundering, needy kiss of a man who wanted her, a man who needed her just as much as she needed him, and she went up on tiptoe to meet him, to search his mouth, her tongue exploring, duelling with his, her hands sliding round under his jacket to press against the warmth of his back and hold him closer. She felt the strong columns of muscle that bracketed his spine, felt them tense, slid her hands lower and felt his buttocks tighten as he rocked against her.

'Alice—'

'Make love to me, Marco,' she murmured, and he held her motionless for a moment, then broke away.

'Not here,' he said gruffly, and took her hand and led her away from the rose terrace, going into the house by a different door, cutting through corridors and passageways she'd never been in, until at last they were in her room.

He turned the heavy iron key in the door but left the light off and the curtains open, so that all they had was the moonlight.

'Now I'm going to do what I should have done before,' he said softly, and taking her in his arms, he kissed her again, the promise sending tiny shockwaves of anticipation through her.

He kissed her gently this time, building the heat slowly until she wanted to scream, and then he stepped away, stripped off his jacket, his tie, his shirt, laying them meticulously on the chair as he heeled off his shoes and peeled away the rest of his clothes.

She'd never seen him naked, but she saw him now, his skin silvered in the moonlight, and it took her breath away. His body was powerful, his limbs long and lean and taut, his chest and abdomen defined by a scatter of hair that arrowed down. Her eyes followed it and fluttered shut on a trembling sigh.

'I need you,' she said, her breath sobbing, but his lips touched hers to silence her, then as he drew away he murmured something in Italian, his voice soothing.

She felt his hands on her again, turning her, finding the button studded with crystals that held the dress together at the nape of her neck. He eased it undone and turned her round again to face him but she kept her eyes closed as he drew the shoulders down, peeling away the sleeves so that the dress slithered off her, leaving her standing only in tiny silky shorts.

She had a ridiculous urge to cross her arms over her breasts, but then she felt his hands cup them and her breath shuddered out on a fragile sigh.

Alice felt him move closer, felt the brush of his thighs, the solid, heavy press of his erection against her belly, the slight rasp of hair as his chest came into contact with hers and his arms closed around her.

She felt one hand slide up her back, felt him thread his fingers into her hair and tug it gently down so that she arched her neck to him. His mouth—hot, soft, gently biting—teased the skin of her throat, his breath drifting over her skin and setting fire to it, his other hand finding a breast and cradling it.

He groaned and said something she couldn't understand, his breath hot against her skin, and his mouth moved on, finding her nipple, but he'd had to move away to do that and she'd lost contact with him.

'Marco—'

She heard the rustle of bedclothes and he lifted her easily and laid her on the bed, coming down beside her and pulling the covers over them to keep her warm.

He touched her everywhere, his mouth following his hands, tormenting every inch of her skin, from the soles of her feet to the delicate skin behind her ear and everything in between, taking her to the brink time and time again until finally she broke and begged him.

'Please, Marco—I need you… Please—'

And then at last he was there, burying himself deep inside her, his mouth on hers, his tongue thrusting in time with his body as the tension tightened until she thought she would die.

And then it rolled through her like the crash of thunder, wave after wave of sensation as the tension broke and shattered into a million pieces, and he caught her scream in his mouth and sobbed her name as his body went rigid. And then he slumped against her, his chest heaving.

'Alice, *tesoro*...'

His mouth found hers again, raining tender kisses on her lips, her eyes, her cheeks, then back to her mouth again for one last, tender caress before he lifted his head and stared down at her, his eyes glittering in the moonlight.

'Oh, Marco,' she whispered, tears flooding her eyes, and he bent his head and kissed them away.

'Don't cry, *tesoro*,' he murmured tenderly.

'I'm not,' she said, and tried to laugh, but she could still feel the aftershocks echoing through their bodies, and the tears fell anyway.

He rolled to his side, taking her with him, and as she settled against him, her head on his shoulder, she touched her lips to his skin.

'I love you,' she said silently, and he might have understood because his arms tightened slightly around her and his lips pressed gently to her forehead.

'Go to sleep, *amore mio*,' he murmured, and she snuggled closer and let her eyes drift shut.

* * *

'I won't ask where you've been.'

Marco stubbed his toe on the end of the bed and swore. 'Good. It's none of your business.'

'No, it isn't. Just a head's up, though. They know she's pregnant.'

Marco found the bedside light and turned it on.

'What are you talking about?'

'Alice, *figlio mio.*'

'I realise that. What on earth makes them think she's pregnant?'

Raffaello laughed. 'She hasn't drunk any alcohol, she's been avoiding all sorts of food—'

'She doesn't drink, and she has a medical condition. She has to be very careful with her diet. It has nothing to do with being pregnant.'

'You're a lousy liar.'

'I'm not lying!'

His brother propped himself up on his pillows and folded his arms. 'Maybe, maybe not. It may be that she does have a medical condition, but she's also pregnant. I guess you didn't want them to know?'

Marco gave up trying to deny it, sat down on the other bed and met his brother's eyes. 'No. I didn't. It's very early, she's had a threatened miscarriage, her medical condition makes it a high-risk pregnancy—and anyway, we're not together, as I keep telling you.'

Raffe laughed at him. 'Well, that's not how it looked in the rose bower, or last night when you were dancing, and it was no surprise to anyone when the two of you slipped out of the marquee and vanished. That looked pretty together, to me.'

Marco shook his head. 'We're not. Or we haven't been, not since—well, whatever. Not really. We're working on it, but tonight was the first time since then, and it's really early days, so say what the hell you like to me but please don't tease her about it.'

His brother frowned. 'You really love her, don't you?'

He hesitated, then nodded, the admission torn from him. 'Yes. Yes, I love her, and I want us to be together, but she's wary, and independent, and she doesn't trust easily, and she won't marry me just because she's pregnant.'

'Have you asked her?'

'No, of course I haven't asked her! We're not that close.'

'You got her pregnant. That's pretty close.'

'That was an accident! A one-off. We got carried away, that's all.'

'I'm not surprised, if she was wearing anything like that dress. It's very revealing, by the way. Nice neat little bump.'

He felt his blood run cold. 'Bump?' He knew she had a bump, he'd felt it last night when he'd made love to her, but—did it show?

'Ah, come on, man! She's stick thin, there's nowhere to hide it, and it may be early, but it didn't go unnoticed.'

He swore and met Raffe's eyes. 'They're going to be all over us tomorrow, aren't they?'

'Absolutely. That's why I'm telling you, just so you're forewarned.'

'Forewarned? I wish I thought that would help. The women in this family could teach the Mafia a thing or two when it comes to inter-rogation.'

'You could always sneak off early without talking to any of them.'

He snorted, although the idea had already crossed his mind. 'No. I haven't said goodbye to Annalisa and Matteo and, anyway, if we run away it'll only fuel the fire. We'll just deny it.'

Raffe laughed. 'Like that'll work.' He glanced at his watch, punched his pillows and lay down again. 'Put that light out and go to sleep. It's five-thirty and I've only been in bed two hours.'

Marco undressed—well, the little he'd both-ered to put on to go from one room to the other—and got into bed, but he couldn't sleep.

Not now, not with the knowledge of what was waiting for them. Although maybe if they were together, his family wouldn't say anything in front of her. Surely not even they would be so crass?

He'd talk to her in the morning, work out what they were going to say.

CHAPTER NINE

THE DAYLIGHT WOKE her gently, and she turned towards Marco with a smile and found he was gone.

Back to his room, so that Raffaello wouldn't realise where he'd been all night? Or in case someone else came to find them in the morning and found his bed untouched?

Whatever, he was gone, and the sheets were cold. She rolled to his side of the bed and breathed in the scent of him, reviving the images of the night. She wanted him, wished he was still there to make love to her again.

Not that he hadn't already. She felt herself smile, and she pulled his pillow into her arms and hugged it.

It had been amazing. Their first time, right after the gala, had been shocking in its intensity, pure and unadulterated hot sex, but this time—both times—it had felt completely different. He'd drawn every nuance out of their lovemaking, and while it had still been hot, still intense, it had been so tender, so gentle, so— *loving.*

And the things he'd said—she hadn't understood the words, but from the way he'd said them, the way he'd touched her, she'd understood the meaning. Or hoped she had.

Had he had a change of heart? Or had she simply misunderstood what he'd felt for her all along? He'd been amazing ever since she'd told him she was pregnant, done all manner of things to make her life easier, tried to take the load off her at work, gone with her to the hospital a fortnight ago when she'd had the scare, held her hand through all the tests, gone with her again—what more could he have done?

Told me he loves me?

He hadn't, hadn't even hinted at it until last night. Sure, he'd been affectionate, but never passionate. Why? Because she'd pushed him away? Or had he pushed her?

She'd been so adamant that she wasn't going to be in a relationship with him simply because she was pregnant, but then although he'd talked about them maybe being together, he'd done nothing to move their relationship forward since then—or had he? Had the times he'd fed her, the times he'd kissed her, been a gentle attempt to strengthen the bond between them and move it on into something deeper and more mean-ingful?

She'd just assumed all that care and atten-tion was because of the baby. She'd pushed him away so many times in so many little ways, but only because she didn't want him to be with her just because she was pregnant. He had to want her for herself, and how could she know that if he didn't tell her?

But maybe he'd tried. Maybe that was how he'd told her that he cared, in all those endlessly thoughtful gestures, the little kindnesses he'd shown her day after day?

She sighed, defeated by the endless circle of her thoughts, and throwing back the bedclothes she got out of bed and went to the bathroom. She needed something to eat soon to stave off the nausea before it got out of hand, and there wouldn't be anyone in the kitchen so early, so she showered quickly, pulled on the clothes she'd travelled in and sent him a text, hoping it would get through.

I need to eat. I'm going down to raid the kitchen. See you soon?

She hesitated, then added an *x* and pressed 'send', then let herself out and crept quietly along the corridor and down the stairs, her ballet flats soundless on the old stone.

She wasn't going to be first in the kitchen, she realised as she approached the door. There were people in there talking and laughing, although it was barely eight o'clock and the music had been playing until at least three in the morning. Still, she needed to eat and she was sure they wouldn't mind.

She'd opened the door and was about to step inside when she heard the sound of running feet and Marco appeared, a little dishevelled, his jeans and sweater tugged on, his feet still bare, his voice urgent.

'Alice, wait—'

'Auguri!'

She stopped dead in the doorway, shocked by the sudden eruption of noise from the women in the room, all smiling and laughing and gathering round them, drawing them in. Marco was at her back, his hands on her shoulders giving them a gentle squeeze, and she could feel the tension coming off him as she heard his name called a dozen times, with laughter and evident happiness.

She turned her head. 'What are they saying?' she said to him, and he shook his head.

'It means congratulations. They know about

the baby,' he said softly, so softly that she barely
heard it over the clamour of voices.

'Congratulations,' his mother said in English, coming over to hug them both. 'I wait
so long for Marco to find someone he really
loves, and now he is having a baby with you. I
am so happy.'

'Thank you,' she said, because it seemed
pointless to deny it, and then everyone was hugging them.

Until Sofia said, 'We need to plan the wedding,' and she felt the words like a bucket of
cold water flung over her head.

'Wedding?' She shook her head dumbly,
forced into a corner and unable to know what
to say or how to respond, but Marco said something in rapid-fire Italian and his mother stepped
back and looked from him to her as if she was
waiting for her response.

But she had no idea what Marco had just told
them, so she said the first thing that came into
her head. 'No, you don't understand, we don't
have any plans—'

'But the baby—it is Marco's baby, yes?'

She couldn't deny it, couldn't lie to them, so
she nodded. 'Yes, of course, but we aren't—he
isn't—'

She turned to him in desperation, but his
eyes were fixed across the room, and she fol-

lowed the direction of his gaze and saw a young woman who'd been at the wedding, one of the guests. She'd been seated near Raffaello and Alice thought she'd seen them dancing, but she was staring at Marco now, a million emotions written all over her face, and then with a shake of her head she put a hand over her mouth and slipped past them out of the room, tears in her eyes.

His head turned, his eyes on her, and she could feel the tension in him like a steel cable about to snap. '*Scusi*,' he said, and pushing past her he followed the girl out, leaving her alone with the women.

No way. She turned and followed them, catching up with Marco in the courtyard. 'Marco, wait. What's going on? Who is she? Why's she crying?'

He stopped and turned to her, his face ravaged by an emotion she didn't understand. 'It's Francesca. The girl I was engaged to. I'm sorry, I have to go to her. I'll come and find you.'

And everything fell into place.

His reluctance to come here for the wedding, the tension she'd felt in him when they'd arrived, his wariness about anyone knowing— all of it, because despite what he'd told her he still loved Francesca, and now it seemed she still loved him.

He wasn't free. His heart was definitely taken, and not by her. She watched him go, sprinting across the courtyard after the woman he loved, and all her hopes crumbled to dust.

She should have known better than to believe in fairy tales. Of course he didn't love her. She drew in a breath, gathered herself together and made her way back up the stairs to her room, the need to get away overwhelming her. His family was in meltdown, Francesca was heartbroken— she had to pack and get out of here before she did any more harm or caused any more grief—

'Alice?'

She turned. Raffaello was standing in the doorway in jeans and a sweater. Unlike Marco he had shoes on, but he'd obviously got straight out of bed. Because Marco had called him?

'They know,' she said, her voice trembling. 'The women. They think we're getting married, and Francesca was upset—'

'Francesca?'

'Yes. He still loves her—he must. He ran after her—I don't know. Raffaello, I need to get to the airport. Will you take me? Please? I should never have come here and I need to go now, before Marco comes back. I can't deal with him, not now.'

'You can't go, Alice, not without talking to him—'

'I can. I have to. I can't talk about this, not here, not now. I just want to go home.'

'I have to tell him—'

'No! Please, Raffaello, no. Don't tell him. Please—just help me. If you can't take me, then please call me a taxi or find someone who can, because I need to go home.'

He looked up at the ceiling, closed his eyes, breathed out and nodded. 'OK. I'll help you. I think you're wrong, but I'll help you to get home. You can talk to him later. Are you ready to go?'

'Yes. I'm all packed.'

'Do you have your ticket?'

She shook her head. 'No, but we weren't going until tonight. I want to go now. I need to—'

'No matter. We can buy a ticket but we need to hurry, there's a flight leaving soon. They might have a seat.'

He dived back into his room, came back with a jacket on and car keys in his hand, and he lifted her case and took her out the way Marco had brought her back in the night before, down the back stairs and out of the side door.

His car was there, and he started the engine and headed down the drive as she was still fastening her seat belt.

It was fast, of course, a sleek, low sports car

with rock hard suspension, probably ridiculously expensive, but he treated it like a hire car, or maybe worse.

It took less than an hour to the airport, and he dropped her off to park the car. By the time he reappeared she was trying to negotiate a seat on the next flight.

He took over, his rapid Italian getting her a ticket for a flight that left in less than an hour.

She was reaching for her purse when he pulled out his wallet, paid for the ticket and handed it to her. 'Here. Have it on me, and get moving. That's the last call for your flight. You get home safely and try not to worry. I'll talk to him, and to Francesca. Don't worry, Alice. It'll be all right.'

Would it? She doubted it. Numb, she boarded the plane and stared out of the window as the ground fell away beneath them.

All right? She couldn't think of any way that it would be all right, any of it, ever again.

Had he got it wrong all this time? Did Cesca still love him?

He rapped on the door. 'Francesca, it's me. I need to talk to you.'

The door opened and Francesca stood there, tears streaking her face.

'Oh, Cesca, I'm sorry,' he said, but she shook her head and hugged him.

'No. No, I'm sorry. Sorry you still can't commit to anyone, still can't let yourself be happy, can't let yourself be the man I know you are inside. I thought you'd finally found someone you could love, someone who loved you, too, but I saw Alice's face today, the way she loves you, the sorrow in her eyes when you didn't acknowledge that.'

She looked up at him, her eyes searching. 'You looked so good together last night, so happy, and I thought, Finally!, and then today—was it all a lie, the way you were with her last night?'

He shook his head, confused by her words. 'No. It wasn't a lie, Cesca, none of it. I do love her, and, yes, we are having a baby.'

'So why didn't you tell them all that instead of yelling at them to leave her alone and saying it was none of their business? Why not commit to her? Doesn't she deserve that?'

He rammed a hand through his hair. 'Of course she does, but it's not like that, we're honestly not together.'

'You were last night and clearly you have been at some point in the past,' she said, in much the same way Raffaello had in the early hours of the morning. 'It's so obvious she loves you—'

'She doesn't trust me, Cesca. She's been badly hurt, but we're getting there, and I'm hopeful, and she's happy for me to be part of the baby's life, if it gets to that point—'

'If?'

He turned to face her, meeting her troubled eyes. 'She's not... She has a condition that makes any pregnancy high risk, and she's already had a bleed two weeks ago. It's all OK, but whether it stays that way, I don't know, but she thinks I only want her for the baby, and it's not true.'

'No, of course it's not true. I know that, but then I know you. You need to be a husband and father, deep down inside you're aching for it, you always have been, but you've always put yourself last and your career first for the sake of other people's children, but you're having your own now, Marco! Surely this time that's more important? Please, don't let this go wrong for you both. I so want you to be happy.'

Another tear ran down Francesca's cheek, and he reached out and wiped it gently away. 'Oh, Cesca, don't cry for me, I'm not worth it.'

'Of course you are! You're a good man, and last night I thought you were finally getting somewhere for the first time since I sent you away.'

'You didn't send me away.'

'Yes, I did, and they all blamed you, and I feel guilty for that.'

He shrugged. 'They had to blame someone, why not me? I was already the black sheep for leaving to follow my dream, it was just another nail in the same coffin. And anyway it wasn't right between us. I would have gone sooner or later.'

She nodded, but her eyes were troubled. 'Marco, there's something you don't know. Raffe and I—after you left, we...'

He frowned at her, stunned as her meaning sank in. 'You and Raffe? But—why didn't he tell me? He would have done, I know that.'

'I asked him not to. We became friends while you and I were still engaged, while you were in England. I was unhappy because I knew you didn't want to settle down in Italy, at least until you'd finished your training, so I told you I wouldn't move to England with you and you ended it, and suddenly my feelings for him crystallised. He was my first lover, Marco—my only lover. It didn't last long, I think because he felt guilty that he might somehow have caused our break-up, but we've been seeing each other again in the last couple of months—nothing serious, not yet, but last night we danced and we talked and—he wants to talk to you today, to tell you about us, ask your blessing—'

'My blessing? Francesca, of course you have my blessing! You and Raffe would be *perfect* together. He's everything I was supposed to be, everything you wanted. How could I possibly mind if you found happiness with each other?'

Her eyes filled with hope. 'Are you sure?'

'Of course I'm sure! Cesca, I need to talk to Alice, to explain why you were crying. When I saw that look on your face I thought you weren't over us, I thought I'd got it wrong when we split up. I would never have guessed this in a million years. I need to explain to her—'

'She's not here,' she told him, looking up from her phone. 'She's with Raffe. He's taking her to the airport.'

'*What?*'

'He's just sent me a text. He said not to tell you. She doesn't want to talk to you and she doesn't want you to follow her.'

'But I have to!'

'You won't catch them. You know how Raffe drives, and there's an early flight. You won't get there in time, Marco, and you don't want to make a scene at the airport.'

He sat down on her bed and dropped his head into his hands, stunned. Alice was leaving him, just when everything was starting to look so good for them. Last night, in bed, she'd been so loving, so tender with him, and he'd finally thought they were getting somewhere, but now—now she was running away from him again. How could it all have gone so wrong?

He felt the bed dip, felt the warmth of Francesca's arm around him, and he straightened up and looked despairingly into her eyes.

'What can I do, Cesca? I love her more than I've ever loved anyone. I'd do anything for her, but she doesn't want to know.'

'Have you asked her?'

'What?'

'Have you asked her? Asked her to marry you?'

He shook his head. 'No. It's too soon.'

'How can it be too soon? She's having your baby! Marco, have you even told her that you love her?'

He let his breath out on a long sigh. 'No. Well, yes. Last night, in her room, but in Italian. I don't know if she understood, but I instinctively said it in Italian because it's the language of my heart, but that was stupid, wasn't it?'

She laughed softly. 'Probably, but communication has never been your strong point. You've never really talked about your feelings. You're just like your father.'

'My father? My father doesn't even *like* me.'

'Of course he does. He loves you to bits, Marco, and he's so proud of you. He's got the profile picture of you from the Hope Hospital website as the screensaver on his phone!'

Really?

He turned back to her, took her hands in his. 'Cesca, I have to go. I need to make this right. I'll send her a text, tell her to wait for me at the airport—'

'No, Marco. Let her go, catch the next flight, and talk to her at home, in private.'

He sighed harshly, angry with himself for not going straight back to Alice in the middle of the night when Raffe had told him they all knew, asking her then to marry him, telling her—in English, for heaven's sake!—that he loved her. 'Yes, you're right. I need to do this privately, and face to face. She deserves what I never gave you either—the truth about how I really feel.'

'In English, though!' Cesca told him, laughing gently at him. 'And don't stop saying it until you're sure she's understood.'

She got to her feet and pulled him up. 'Come on, you need to get your shoes on and come into the kitchen, have some breakfast and get on your way. And you need to say goodbye to Annalisa before you go.'

'And Raffe. I need to talk to him—give him

my blessing. I hope you find happiness together, Cesca. I've been so worried about you.'

'No more worried than I've been about you. I did love you, you know, just not enough to fight for you. If I'd loved you enough to last a lifetime, I would have followed you anywhere in the world.'

'Would you follow Raffaello?'

She smiled, her eyes filled with love. 'Yes. I would follow him to hell and back, Marco.'

'Does he know that?'

She smiled again. 'Not yet. But he will, as soon as he gets back. So—first things first. Let's get some breakfast.'

Alice let herself into her house, dropped her bag on the floor, ran upstairs, stripped off her clothes and stepped into the shower, standing motionless under the steady stream of hot water.

She felt numb, numb and empty, reamed out inside, but as the water warmed her the feeling came back, and pain swamped her. Her chest heaved, then heaved again, and she slumped against the wall and sobbed her heart out.

She should never have trusted him! It had taken so long for her to give in, and as soon as she had, as soon as she'd decided she could trust him, he'd betrayed that trust, because he was still in love with another woman and everything he'd said and done to and for her was all about the baby.

'You're a fool,' she told herself. 'A stupid, stupid fool.'

And then she straightened up, pulled herself together, washed her hair, her body... Her hands lingered over the slight swelling low down in her abdomen, over the fullness of her breasts. Her body was changing. It wouldn't be long before everyone would know.

Well, she could deal with that. She'd dealt with worse. Working with Marco would be worse, but maybe it wouldn't come to that. Maybe he'd change his mind and go back to Italy, to Francesca who obviously still loved him. And from the way he'd run after her, it was obvious he still loved her, too.

So much for all those tender endearments in the night.

She gritted her teeth, washed herself properly and then towelled herself dry, pulled on clean clothes, did her hair, her make-up, and went to work.

There were people there who needed her, vulnerable sick children. She'd had enough time out, and look where it had got her. Time to get back to reality.

* * *

'So, you're all better, Daisy. I'm so pleased. Would you like to go home soon?'

The little girl nodded, her eyes bright with excitement.

'Can I? Can I really?'

'Yes, I think you can.' She turned to Olive. 'Is that OK with you? She can go either today or tomorrow morning, whichever suits you better.'

'Today would be wonderful! Dan's taking some time off work, so he's only going to be doing the mornings, and—oh, here he is. Dan, Daisy can come home today!'

'Oh, that's fantastic,' he said, hugging his daughter in a way that left no doubt in anyone's mind how much he loved her. 'That's fantastic,' he said again, and Alice could hear his voice was choked.

Her own would be, too, because all she could think of was her baby and how Marco would feel every time he said goodbye and flew back to Francesca without his child. How she would feel every time it was his turn to have the child for Christmas, or a birthday, or some other celebration.

She blinked away the tears and got back to business.

'Right, if you're all happy about that I'll go and write your discharge letter and then you're free to go.'

'Can I say goodbye to Marco?'

Marco. 'Daisy, I'm sorry, he's not here today, but I'll come down to see you off. I'll be about an hour, that's all.'

She went to her office and the first thing she saw was Marco's stethoscope lying on the desk. The stethoscope Daisy had been listening to his heart with when it had speeded up. Because she'd arrived on the scene?

Nonsense. It was nothing to do with it, and if it was, it was all about sexual attraction and nothing to do with loving her. He didn't love her. If he'd loved her he wouldn't have abandoned her like that with his entire family and gone to Francesca.

She put the stethoscope in a drawer out of sight, put him out of her mind and turned on her computer. Twenty minutes later she'd written the discharge letter, sent a copy to file, another to Daisy's GP and tucked a hard copy into an envelope for the Lawrences, and checked her emails.

Dozens of them. She deleted a lot, read others, replied to a few, left some for later and went to see Daisy off.

* * *

She wasn't at home, but he could see through the letterbox that she'd arrived because her flight bag was on the floor in the hall.

Her car was missing, too. Had she gone to work?

Probably.

He logged into the hospital site and checked the emails to see if there were any sent by her, and found two he'd been copied into by default. Right. So she was there. Good.

He drove to the hospital, parked his car at the front and walked between the huge, sparkling Christmas trees and into the foyer, and there she was, talking to Dan and Olive Lawrence. It looked like Daisy was going home, and she'd seen him, so he had no choice but to talk to her, to say goodbye.

Not what he'd planned, but at least he'd found Alice, and he wasn't letting her walk away from him this time.

'It's Marco!'

Alice felt her heart thud, and then he strode through the doors and walked up to her. She'd never seen him look so deadly serious and determined, and she swallowed.

'Did you want me?' she asked as he reached them, and something flashed in his eyes.

'Yes, I want you, but we can talk about that in a minute,' he said, his voice laced with hidden meaning. 'We need to say goodbye to Daisy first.'

He crouched down and held out his arms, and Daisy threw herself at him and hugged him hard. 'I thought you weren't coming to say goodbye to me,' she said, and he hugged her back and then let go and straightened up.

'Of course I've come to say goodbye. I'm so glad you're better, Daisy, you and Wuzzle.'

She held Wuzzle up to him, and he kissed the teddy goodbye and handed him back before shaking hands with Dan and Olive.

'Thank you,' Dan said. 'Thank you both for everything you've done for Daisy, and for us. I just—there aren't words—'

'You don't need to thank us,' Alice told them, hugging them both with a huge lump in her throat. 'Seeing you together with Daisy well is all the thanks we need. And you'll be back in Outpatients in January for Daisy's check-up, so have a wonderful Christmas together, and we'll see you soon.'

She watched them walk out through the doors, then, her heart in her mouth, she turned to Marco.

'Not here,' he said. 'My house, now.'

'But I'm at work—'

'Not any more, Alice. Not today. You're not on the rota, neither am I, and we need to talk. My car's just here.'

'I can't—'

'Yes, you can, Alice, because this won't wait and I'm not going to let you run away again. There are things I need to say to you, things I should have said long ago, and I'm not waiting any longer.'

'I have emails—'

'Of course you do. You'll always have emails, and patients, and results and admin and meetings, but not now. Not today. Today, we talk.'

She opened her mouth, shut it and nodded, because he was right, those things would always be there, and if nothing else they needed to clear the air so they could both move on with their lives.

Swallowing back tears, she followed him out to his car in a silence that wasn't broken until they'd walked through his front door.

'So,' she said when they reached the sofa by the garden doors, 'you wanted to talk, so talk.'

She wasn't going to make it easy, but that didn't surprise him. Nothing about Alice was ever easy. Nevertheless, he wasn't going to let her off the hook so he put the ball back in her court.

'Why did you run away this morning?'

Her eyes flicked away. 'I didn't run—'

'You ran. Raffe said you couldn't get away fast enough and you wouldn't let him tell me where you were, wouldn't talk to me yourself, just wanted to get home. Why?'

'Why? You heard them, Marco! All those women, clamouring for some idealistic happy-ever-after when all the time you were still in love with Francesca—'

'No! I'm not in love with her! I've never been in love with her. I love her, sure, but I've *never* been in love with her and she's never loved me, not the way she loves Raffe and he loves her.'

She turned her head and stared at him. 'Raffe? Francesca and Raffaello?'

'That's exactly what I thought, but they're perfect for each other. He's the son I should have been, the husband she needs, and she's the woman he wants. Apparently they had an affair years ago, right after I broke up with her, but just briefly, and now they've been seeing each other again, but they didn't know how to tell me. They're getting married, Alice. He proposed to her right after I left.'

'So—why was she crying?'

'Because she was sad for me, because even though everything between us looked right the night before, this morning we denied that we were together, and she thought it was because I was still running away from commitment, that after all this time I still wasn't letting myself be happy, still putting medicine first before my personal life. I didn't talk to her at the wedding—I think she was keeping out of my way, and this morning—well, you saw what happened this morning.'

She was silent for a minute, and then she looked back at him. 'Why did they all jump to conclusions about us?'

'Because they could see how we felt about each other! We didn't exactly keep it secret, and they could all see that you're pregnant. They could see how much I love you, Alice, and they could see that you love me. And you do love me, don't you?'

It wasn't really a question, and she didn't answer it, at least not in so many words. Instead she turned it round.

'You don't love me, Marco. You're only saying it now because you're afraid if you don't, you won't be with the mother of your child. I saw you with Daisy today. You love children, and I watched the way you said goodbye to her. How much harder would it be if it was your own child you were saying goodbye to, over and over again, because you couldn't be together as a family? So of course you're telling me you love me, because you want to be near your child and that's the only way you can achieve it.'

He sat down on the sofa, and pulled her down beside him. She sat stiffly on the edge, keeping herself contained, buttoned up as only Alice could, and it made his heart ache.

'Why do you believe you're so unlovable, Alice?' he asked softly. 'Why is it so hard to believe that I love you with all my heart? You're the light in my darkness, the sun to brighten my day, the reason I wake up in the mornings, the person I long for at night. *Ti amo, carissima mia.* I love you. I will always love you, as long as my heart's beating, as long as I'm breathing, and nothing you can say will change that.'

She sucked in her breath, glanced at him quickly and looked away again.

'You're just saying that. It's just words, Marco, pretty words to fool me. I'm not going to stop you having access to your baby—'

'This is *not* about our baby,' he said, cutting her off. 'This is about you, and me, and what we feel. When you had that bleed, my first thought was for you. That you should be safe, not bleed to death, not lose the baby that meant so much to you, the baby you'd never thought you'd have. It was never about the baby for me, Alice. It's *never* been about the baby. It's *always* been about you.'

'You're just saying that,' she said again, but he could hear something in her voice, something unbearably sad that told him she wanted to believe him, desperately wanted to believe him, but simply couldn't.

'No,' he said, sliding off the edge of the sofa onto his knees and taking her hands in his, waiting for her eyes to meet his.

'Look at me, *tesoro*. Do I look as if I'm just saying this? I. Love. You. *Ti amo*, Alice. *Sei l'amore della mia vita.* You're the love of my life, the only woman I've ever, ever loved like this, so much that it hurts. *Mi vuoi sposare?* Will you marry me, Alice? Marry me, and make me the happiest man alive?'

'What if I lose the baby? You won't want me then.'

He shook his head and sighed in exasperation. 'Of course I will, and I will *cry* with you, *bella,* but I'll still love you, and I'll still be there for you, because I can't help myself from loving you. I told you that last night—said all of this, but I did it wrong, I said it in Italian, instinctively, because it means more to me than it does in English. If I speak in Italian it comes from my heart, and I wanted to tell you these things from my heart, not my brain, not in translation, but from my soul, *amore mio. Ti amo,* Alice. Now and for ever. I love you.'

He stared into her eyes, willing her to believe him, willing her to dare to trust him, and then slowly, bit by bit, he saw the hope dawn in their depths, the blue, always bright, turn brilliant ultramarine as the sun slanted in and caught the tears that shimmered in her eyes.

'Oh, Marco,' she said, and then she slid to her knees and cradled his face in her hands. 'I love you, too, so much. I thought you were just—I don't know. I was so confused, but I couldn't believe that you loved me that much, that anyone could love me that much.'

His hands came up and cupped her face. 'Why? What's not to love, Alice? You're beautiful in every way—the care you give the children entrusted to us by their parents is incredible, their lives so infinitely precious to you. I've seen you cry when they hurt, laugh when they're happy, grieve when they die. I've seen you take the load off colleagues to give them time to be with their families, I've heard you talking to your mother, your concern for your family, concern for everyone but yourself.

'You always put yourself last, try not to be a burden, deny yourself happiness—you didn't even stay and fight for me when I went after Francesca!'

'No, because I thought you still loved her. I thought I'd lost you—no, that I'd never really had you. You'd never told me you loved me, never asked me to be with you, to be part of your life—'

'That's not true. I've asked you to stay over, I've asked you to come for a meal so I can cook for you—I've done it countless times—'

'To keep the baby safe.'

'No! To keep you safe, to make you happy, to care for you the way you care for everyone. But every time, or almost every time, you say no and push me away. I'm a proud man, Alice. I wasn't going to grovel, but it didn't stop me loving you, and it never will. My heart belongs to you.'

She smiled tenderly up at him, her hand sliding down to rest right in the centre of his chest. 'Then I'd better take care of it, and you'd better take care of mine, Marco, because although I didn't dare to believe you would really want it, it's been yours ever since we met. I love you. I love you so much. And, yes, please.'

He frowned, not entirely certain… 'Yes?'

'Yes, I'll marry you, but only if you promise to teach me enough Italian that I can understand when you tell me something that really, really matters.'

He closed his eyes, squeezing the lids tightly shut to hold back the tears of joy, but then he gave up and opened them and stared down at her. His lover. His friend. And soon to be his wife.

'Lesson one,' he said. '*Baciami*. It means kiss me.'

'*Baciami*,' she repeated, and he smiled.

'I thought you'd never ask,' he murmured.

She laughed softly, the sound like music in his ears, and lifting her face to his she met him halfway...

EPILOGUE

Christmas, one year later...

'*Buon Natale*, Mamma.'

Alice opened her eyes and saw Marco standing over her with a smile, their baby Sophia snuggled in his arms.

'Merry Christmas, my darlings,' she said with a smile, and reached up for a kiss from both of them.

'Your baby wants her *mamma*,' he said, and perched on the edge of the bed as she wriggled up and leant against the pillows. He handed Sophia over so she could feed her, and stayed there as the baby suckled, the tenderness in his eyes filling her heart with happiness as it did every day.

'Is anyone else awake?'

He chuckled. 'Absolutely. Our parents are up, and some of the children, and Raffe and Francesca will be here soon. You've had a lie-in. It's nearly eight.'

'Eight? I need to get up! My family—'

'Are fine. All the parents are in the kitchen with Annalisa and Matteo and the baby, and I could hear children running round in the courtyard. Here, give me Sophia so you can get up—and Sophia and I will go and change that nappy, won't we, *bellissima*?'

'Hmm. Sometimes I think you love her more than me,' she teased, but he turned and shook his head.

'No, *bella mia. Sei l'amore della mia vita.*'

She chuckled. 'I'm not convinced I *am* the love of your life, but you can spend today trying to convince me, if you like.'

He snorted softly, chivvied her into the shower and took the baby away so she could get dressed in peace. Twenty minutes later she found them all in the kitchen—Marco's parents Sofia and Riccardo, his beloved Nonna, who was bouncing Sophia on her knee, Raffe and Francesca, married now for six months and expecting their first baby in April, Annalisa and Matteo with their brand-new baby Giorgio, her parents, her brothers and their wives and the children, all gathered together to celebrate not only Christmas but their first wedding anniversary.

Their wedding had been a quiet celebration in Cambridge the previous year, followed by

Christmas with his family and hers, and now they were all back together again, gathered round the huge kitchen table that was piled with the traditional pastries and little tarts, the air sweet with the scent of toasted *panettone* and freshly brewed coffee and the trill of excited little voices.

'Alice, look!' they chorused, and her nephews and nieces almost fell over themselves to show her what they were eating.

'Cappuccino, *bella mia*,' Marco said, putting the coffee down in front of her and stealing a kiss before handing her the baby. 'I'll make you some scrambled eggs.'

'Thank you,' she said, knowing his family understood now how important it was to her to keep her body balanced, because little Sophia had opened her eyes to a love she'd never hoped to experience, and they both wanted another child.

But for now she wasn't pregnant, and the coffee smelt amazing so she was going to enjoy it while she had the chance.

'*Buon Natale*, everyone,' she said, and raised her cup to them. 'Merry Christmas!'

* * * * *

Welcome to the
Hope Children's Hospital quartet!

Their Newborn Baby Gift
by Alison Roberts
One Night, One Unexpected Miracle
by Caroline Anderson

Available now!

And next month, look out for

The Army Doc's Christmas Angel
by Annie O'Neil
The Billionaire's Christmas Wish
by Tina Beckett